A DINNER TO DIE FOR

Center Point Large Print

This Large Print Book carries the Seal of Approval of N.A.V.H.

A DINNER TO DIE FOR

CLAUDIA
BISHOP

CENTER POINT PUBLISHING
THORNDIKE, MAINE

This Center Point Large Print edition
is published in the year 2006 by arrangement with
The Berkley Publishing Group, a division of
Penguin Group (USA) Inc.

The text of this Large Print edition is unabridged. In other aspects, this book may vary from the original edition. Printed in Thailand. Set in 16-point Times New Roman type.

ISBN 1-58547-843-1

Library of Congress Cataloging-in-Publication Data

Bishop, Claudia, 1947-
A dinner to die for / Claudia Bishop. -- Center Point large print ed.
p. cm.
ISBN 1-58547-843-1 (lib. bdg. : alk. paper)
1. Quilliam, Meg (Fictitious character)--Fiction. 2. Quilliam, Quill (Fictitious character)--Fiction. 3. Hemlock Falls (N.Y. : Imaginary place)--Fiction. 4. Women detectives--New York (State)--Fiction. 5. Murder--Investigation--Fiction. 6. Sisters--Fiction. 7. Hotels--Fiction. 8. Large type books. I. Title.

PS3552.I75955D56 2006
813'.54--dc22

2006011101

For
Peg Homburger
and Janet LeFervre

CAST OF CHARACTERS

THE INN AT HEMLOCK FALLS

Sarah "Quill" Quilliam	manager and owner
Margaret "Meg" Quilliam	her sister, chef and owner
Doreen Muxworthy-Stoker	head housekeeper
Dina Muir	receptionist and PhD candidate
John Raintree	business consultant
Kathleen Kiddermeister	head waitress
Mike Santini	head groundskeeper
Bjarne Bjarnson	head chef
Leo "Boom-Boom" Maltby	guest and entrepreneur
Sheree Maltby	guest and ecdysiast
Brittney-Anne Maltby	guest and ecdysiast
Taffi	guest and ecdysiast
Candi	guest and ecdysiast
Norwood Ferguson	guest and entrepreneur
Mr. Kelvin	guest
Max	dog

And various waiters, waitresses, and sous chefs.

RESIDENTS OF HEMLOCK FALLS

Myles McHale	sheriff and investigator
Davy Kiddermeister	deputy sheriff
Elmer Henry	mayor of Hemlock Falls
Adela Henry	the mayor's wife
Marge Schmidt	businesswoman
Betty Hall	Marge's partner
Dookie Shuttleworth	minister
Axminster Stoker	newspaper publisher
Howie Murchison	town attorney and justice
Esther West	owner, West's Best Dress Shoppe
Carol Ann Spinoza	tax assessor
Harvey Bozzel	president, Bozzel Advertising
Harland Peterson	president of the Agway
Andy Bishop	pediatric internist
Ferris Rodman	builder, the Resort at Hemlock Falls
Jerry Grimsby	chef, owner of Seasons in the Sun
Angela Stoner	news anchor
Bernie MacAvoy	retired farmer

And others

PROLOGUE

Leo "Boom-Boom" Maltby's ex-wife Sheree didn't have a lot in the brains department, but she sure knew her Lincoln Continentals. Leo rested his buttocks comfortably against the sleek black trunk and contemplated the special-order bronze trim with real appreciation. Sheree'd been pretty reasonable about the divorce settlement, considering. He got the Lincoln, and the custom-stretch Hummer, too. It'd crossed his mind more than once that he shouldn't have been so quick to trade Sheree in for Brittney-Anne. Once in a while, something nasty flickered behind Brittney-Anne's turquoise blue eyes. It made the back of his neck itch.

Leo's view of the prospect before him was considerably less affectionate than his wistful memories of Sheree: there were too many flippin' trees. That was the trouble with the country. He liked asphalt. He felt safe with concrete. All kinds of stuff could be hiding in the long grass by the river, among the thick stands of oak and mountain ash. Bears. Wolves. That big hairy guy, whatdyacallit: Sasquatch.

And his flippin' cigar was going out in this flippin' country breeze. He wriggled backwards, plunged his hand into his trouser pocket and withdrew his gold lighter. He heard the car pull off the road and park behind him, but he didn't look around. "You're late, jerkface," he said around the stump of the Monte

Cristo. "Sun's almost down." He flicked the lighter shut. "So whaddya think of the site?"

Footsteps crunched in the gravel behind him.

Leo contemplated the trees and let loose a comfortable belch. "Thing is, with that fancy new resort all ready to open down river, I figure we gotta get moving. This little town's ready to bust wide open. Place like Hemlock Falls, I figured, licensing's gonna be no sweat, and was I right, or what? It's a helluva good idea, come to think on it. These hick farmers'd line up six deep to see the girls. And if the rumors about the gambling casino turn out to be more than just smoke, we could go whole hog here. Topless bar, bottomless bar, your adult film section. Maybe even a toy store for the hick farmers' wives. Some good eats, cheap. I got a classy name for it, too." He spread one thick, hairy hand in a wide arc. "Lovejoy's Nudie Bar and Grill. Pretty good, huh? You could take out them trees, so everyone can see the neon a mile away. Thing is, that flippin' barn's gotta go, first thing. We got to get the locals' attention. I figure we burn the son of a bitch." He turned.

"Oh, yes," said the voice behind him. "We're going to burn the son of a bitch."

The sound of a gunshot seconds later was carried away by the breeze.

CHAPTER 1

The fire horn jerked Sarah Quilliam out of a deep sleep, the kind of sleep where you wake with no sense of who you are or where you've been. She sat straight up in bed, her heart pounding.

"Close your eyes," Myles said. "I'm going to turn on the light."

She fumbled for him in the bedclothes. "Myles?"

"Right here." He was standing at the window. Quill swung her feet to the floor and stood up. Myles turned, reached behind her and flicked on the bedside lamp. Quill rubbed her eyes and tugged at her hair to wake herself up. "There's a fire in town," she said intelligently.

"Mmm." Myles pulled on his chinos and sweatshirt. The sweatshirt was dark gray, with THE INN AT HEMLOCK FALLS on the front in small silver letters. Quill had let Harvey Bozzel, president of Hemlock Falls' best (and only) advertising agency talk her into buying promotional items. The Inn was littered with hats, tee-shirts, sweatshirts and tote bags, all dark gray with silver letters proclaiming the existence of the place, even though Quill thought it would be very hard for anyone to ignore the existence of a forty-thousand-square-foot mansion sprawling on the lip of Hemlock Gorge.

She joined Myles at the window. Her suite of rooms was at the back of the Inn, overlooking the vegetable garden where her sister Meg grew peppers, tomatoes, dill, parsley, and goodness knew what else, so that she could provide their guests with the best food within three hundred miles of the village. Beyond the gardens was a thick stand of trees, and beyond that, a dull orange glow that looked like sunrise. It was August, and the window was open to the warm night. A scent of burning wood drifted through the air. Burning wood, and something else. She glanced at the clock on the bedside table. "It's four o'clock," she said. "In the morning."

Myles kissed the top of her head. "So it is." He sat on the edge of the bed and pulled on his shoes. Quill yawned, then moved to her dresser and fumbled through the drawers for a pair of jeans and a tee-shirt.

"No need to get up," he said. "Go back to sleep."

Quill tugged her jeans over her hips and yawned again. "I'll make coffee and bring it out to wherever it is." She blinked. "As a matter of fact, where is it? The only thing in back of those trees is the old MacAvoy barn. And that's been falling down for years." She pulled her tee-shirt over her head. "I heard MacAvoy sold it. Is that true?"

The phone rang and she jumped at the sudden noise. Myles picked it up. From his side of the conversation, Quill guessed it was Davy Kiddermeister, Myles' deputy sheriff when Myles was in town and sheriff *de facto* when he wasn't.

Myles hung up, pulled open the nightstand drawer, removed his shoulder holster and gun, and put it on.

“Hey,” Quill said, alarmed. “What’s that for? What’s going on?” She shoved her feet into her sandals. “I’m going with you.”

He shrugged into his jacket. “No,” Myles said.

“What do you mean, no?” Quill said indignantly. “You don’t take your gun unless there’s a problem. And if there’s a problem . . .”

“It’s not a matter for civilians.” Myles kissed her again and headed out of the bedroom. Quill hurried after him. She caught up with him at the front door. “It is *really* rotten of you just to take off and leave me to wring my hands and wonder if you’re going to come home flat on a barn door carried by grieving deputies.”

He laughed at that. When Myles laughed, his face softened and caught at her heart. He was fifty-two to Quill’s thirty-six, and a hard life in law enforcement had left its mark. Quill had met very few cops in her life, but those she had met were alike in their detachment and their emotional reserve. She and Myles had come a long way together and she valued the reserve more often than not. But there had been times when that hadn’t been true.

“If it’s the MacAvoy barn—did Davy say it was the MacAvoy barn? There’s nothing out there but trees and woodchucks.”

The phone rang again. Quill reached over the kitchen counter to the wall phone and Myles walked out the door before she could pester him for an answer.

“Rats,” Quill said into the phone.

"Rats to you, too," her sister said. "Is Myles there?"

"Meg. What are you doing up? Are you here?" Quill stretched the phone to the farthest link of the cord, opened the front door and peered into the hall. Meg's small apartment was across the hall from hers, but Meg was rarely there. She spent most of the time at Andy Bishop's. And of course, after next week, Meg wasn't going to be there at all. Quill bit her lip.

"If I were there, I could walk across the hall instead of calling you," Meg pointed out. "I'm with Andy. Except I'm not with Andy, because Davy Kiddermeister called a few seconds ago and said there was a body in the MacAvoy barn, and the MacAvoy barn was burning down to the ground. So Andy grabbed his bag and left. Is Myles there?"

A loud beep sounded on the line. "Just a second, Meggie." Quill tapped the phone button twice to take the waiting call and said hello.

"Myles there?" a cross, elderly voice demanded.

Quill closed the front door, walked back to her small kitchen, and hoisted herself onto the counter. "Good morning to you, too, Doreen."

Doreen Muxworthy-Stoker, the Inn's housekeeper for almost as long as Quill and Meg had owned it, went "t'uh," and said, "Where's the sher'f?"

"Off to the fire," Quill said succinctly.

"So where *is* the fire? Stoke wants to know. Mayor gave him a call, but he was all upset and hung up before Stoke could get the address."

Doreen's third husband—or perhaps it was her fourth,

Quill wasn't entirely certain—was editor-publisher of the *Hemlock Falls Gazette*, the town's best (and only) weekly newspaper.

"It's the MacAvoy barn, I think," Quill said. Doreen slammed the receiver down. Quill sighed, tapped the phone button twice and said, "Meg?"

"I hate it when you just ignore me like that," Meg said furiously. "I hate call-waiting, too. It's rude."

"It's cheaper than having more than one residence line." Quill tucked the phone between her shoulder and her ear to free her hands to make coffee. If she was going to be up at four o'clock in the morning, she was going to be caffeinated to the gills.

"Which reminds me." Meg's voice rose to an indignant squeak. "Dina said you told her to book my rooms. Are we that broke? Are times that tough that you have to kick me out of my own house?"

"We aren't that broke, we're being provident in case the economy gets worse. Your rooms are booked for week after next, Meg. In case you've forgotten, there's a wedding in three days. Yours. To Andy Bishop. And in case you've forgotten that, too, we *did* talk about when your rooms would be free for guests, and you said it would be okay."

There was a short silence. "I don't remember a thing about that."

Quill didn't respond to this for a moment. She poured water into the Cuisinart coffeemaker, then shook a measure of beans straight from the bag into the grinder attachment. The bag was labeled ORANGE SEVILLE in

Meg's clear, spiky handwriting, and the scent of oranges and vanilla perfumed the air. "Are you up?" she asked, finally.

"What do you mean, am I up? Of course I'm up. I'm talking to you, aren't I?"

"I mean up, up. Are you going back to bed? Because if you aren't, I think you should come over here."

"I've got a ton of stuff to do this morning." Meg's voice was sulky.

"What kind of stuff?" Quill punched the on button. The grinder shrieked and she moved out of the kitchen into her living room to get away from the noise. "Bjarne's handling breakfasts this week. And Jerry Grimsby's coming in this afternoon to, you know, help out." Quill felt her voice falter and gave herself a mental shake. It didn't help. Meg had taken a total, irrational, violent dislike to Jerry Grimsby. Jerry Grimsby was Meg's own choice to second her in the kitchen while she went off on her honeymoon with Andy Bishop, Hemlock Fall's best (and only) pediatric internist. "Remember? He's taking over while you're on your honeymoon. He's here to run the kitchen and he's ready to rock and roll. You don't need to do a thing." Quill said this firmly. She had temporarily abandoned taking managerial courses at the Cornell School of Hotel Management in favor of a personal development course at the Ithaca College's Extension Division of Adult Education. This particular personal development course was titled "Face the Music! Counteracting Manners." Its basic premise was that good manners consisted of little white lies. Little white lies got you into more trouble than was psychologically healthy. Truth was better in the long run. The homework assignment for the week was to state the obvious calmly, kindly, firmly, and without bias. Quill cleared her throat. The silence on the other end of the line was so profound she couldn't be sure Meg was breathing. She'd had her doubts about this course, anyway. "Meg?" she said cautiously. "Are you okay? Are you . . ."

The receiver slammed in her ear. Quill hung up thoughtfully and replaced the phone on the wall. As soon as she did so, it rang again. She stared at it. Her best guess was that Meg wanted to start the conversation all over again. She picked it up and said cheerfully, "Hey!"

"Why don't you come over here?" Meg was just as cheerful. So she'd been right. Life was a lot easier when Meg avoided the obvious.

"Gosh. I'd love to. But Dina won't be in to handle the reception desk until nine, and Doreen's off with Stoke at the fire." She yawned. "And I've got a couple of meetings. The Chamber of Commerce and then the Resort Gala Committee." She thought about this for a minute. "You know what? I'm on too many committees."

"That's because you're a wimp," Meg said, momentarily dropping the cheerful-bride act. "A pushover."

Quill didn't say anything. With Meg, it was sometimes better to let the silence stretch.

"So you're stuck. Fine." Meg said in an ominous way. "Me, too. Everybody wants a piece of my time today. You know how it is when you've got a marriage coming up in a few days. Oh, sorry, of course you don't. Well. Busy, busy, busy. See you later, then."

"Right."

"Right."

As far as Quill could tell, they'd both hung up at the same time. She scowled at the wall, picked up the phone and dialed Meg's number. It rang so many times, Quill started to count the rings. Finally, just as she'd decided to hang up, drive over to Andy's house, and shake some sense into her aggravating little sister, Meg picked up.

"You don't have a thing to do for the wedding," Quill said. "Not a thing. This is a quiet, family ceremony, remember? The out-of-town guests are staying here. The reception and the food for the reception are being taken care of here. Jerry Grimsby is handling all of it. And in case you had forgotten, we do this kind of thing for a living. We're *all* handling all of it. All you have to do is put on the dress we bought in Ithaca and *show up!* You're supposed to be spending some time with Andy. We planned it this way, remember?"

"Can I tell you something?" Meg asked in a chatty, confiding way. "Andy's busy, too. Too busy to take a look at that house near Ithaca I want to buy. Too busy to come home tonight to eat the dinner I spent planning *all day yesterday.*"

"He's a doctor, Meg. He can't just walk off in the

middle of emergencies. I thought you guys had worked through this." Quill yawned. "Grow up a little, sweetie. Get a sense of proportion. This is a panic attack, nothing more."

"Proportion, huh?"

"Yes. Not to mention a perfectly understandable panic attack."

"Can I tell you something else?"

"Sure."

"That course you're taking in losing your manners is working."

Quill thought about hanging up again, but didn't. Instead, she took a deep breath and said meekly, "I'm sorry."

"I mean, it's not enough that I'm giving up everything I've ever worked for in this life to some jerkola chef from a lousy two-star restaurant in Ithaca . . ."

"You like Jerry Grimsby. At least you did until last week. Now you've decided he's a cross between Josef Stalin and Idi Amin?"

"He's sneaky," Meg said bitterly. "That whole nice-guy act is a hoax."

"Sneaky?" Quill said. "Jerry Grimsby's the least sneaky person I know. I don't know one single person who doesn't think Jerry's a peach!"

"Everyone's going to like him a lot better than they like me. *He's* not going to cost you a tidy sum in sauté pans every month, is he?"

This was undeniable. Meg's favorite missile in her kitchen was the eight-inch sauté pan that hung over the prep table. The Inn had a standing order for replacements every month.

"And he's so good-tempered, you thought he was on Prozac. You can call me a lot of nice things," (Quill wasn't about to, at the moment) "but you can't call me even-tempered." The bitterness had been replaced by resignation. The resignation alarmed Quill. Resignation was really unlike Meg. Her sister was born contentious. If there was a contention DNA gene, Meg had double the usual number.

"So everyone's going to like him better than they like me. And when I get back from the honeymoon, I. Won't. Have. A. Job."

"Meg, stop crying."

"You're not going to let me back in my own kitchen."

Quill laughed in the warm, comforting way that you laugh when a little kid's just told you there's an alien monster in the closet. "So that's it. Meg, not only are you a part owner of this Inn, you're my favorite sister."

"You don't *have* another sister."

"There's no way that someone like Jerry Grimsby can take your place. There's no way I would *let* Jerry Grimsby take your place, unless, of course, you want him to. Suppose you get pregnant right away? You won't want to work up until the last minute, and guess what? There's good old Jerry Grimsby ready to give you a hand. Suppose . . ."

Meg's voice rose in an hysterical spiral. "I don't even know this guy!"

"Of course you do," Quill said bracingly. "You've

known him since you both trained at the Cordon Bleu. We flew out to San Diego to see his restaurant there, and we loved it. He gave us a tour of his new restaurant in Ithaca and you loved that, too."

"Of course I know Jerry!" Meg shrieked. "I'm talking about Andy!"

"Oh," Quill said. Then, "I see."

Then, "So you'll come over? We'll talk about it?"

"Sure," Meg said miserably.

Quill made two decisions after she hung up the phone. The first was that she'd meet Meg downstairs in the kitchen and put her to work making coffee and food to take to the firefighters. The MacAvoy barn was old and dry and filled with hay and straw. It would have gone up like the tinderbox it was, and the volunteer firefighters would be exhausted. Besides, there was nothing like work as an antidote to pre-wedding nerves. The second decision was to move Meg out of Andy's house and back into her old rooms at the Inn. The second-best antidote to pre-wedding nerves was the familiar. For the next few days, the two of them would go back to the way it was when they had first opened the Inn together. They'd talk over the day's events each evening, curled up in Quill's serene living room, sipping a glass of wine. Myles could go back to his own house for the next few days. He would understand. Myles always understood.

She washed her face, gave her hair a hasty swipe with the brush, pinned it carelessly on top of her head, and jogged down the two flights of stairs to the foyer. The

Inn was full of tourists taking in the last of the summer, and Quill had half-expected a few phone calls to the front desk inquiring about the fire alarm. Mike Santini, who handled night-manager duties when the Inn was full, in addition to his year-round duties as groundskeeper, hadn't left any messages for her at the mahogany reception desk. But there was a note, "Off to the fire," which she'd expected. Like most of the male residents of Hemlock Falls between the ages of eighteen and eighty, Mike was a volunteer fireman. Quill set the phones to ring in the kitchen, then flipped the master switch for all the lights downstairs. She went behind the desk and into her office and flipped the lights on there, too. Mike stretched out on her office couch when he pulled night duty, and he'd left the sheets and blankets in a tangle on the carpeted floor. She folded the linens and stored them in her credenza, went back to the foyer, and through the dining room to the kitchen.

Early mornings at the Inn were her least favorite time of day. The dining tables were bare of tablecloths and flowers. The chairs were tipped up against the tables to give the housekeeping staff room for vacuuming. The wine rack was barred and locked, and the faint scent of the disinfectant used on the kitchen floors hung on the air.

The kitchen was almost as forlorn. But fresh bundles of dill, cilantro, and basil hung drying from the wooden beams, and the Sub-Zeros lining the east wall hummed in a reassuring way. Quill threw the bolt to open the back door, and set coffee cups on the birch prep table. She was rummaging in the wooden bins next to the cobblestone fireplace for coffee beans when the back door whacked open. Meg came in, her short dark hair tousled and her clogs clacking on the slate floor. Quill darted a quick look at her socks. Meg's socks were a good indicator of her current mood. She wore a pair Quill hadn't seen before—a confused, swirly pattern of gray and black. Other than the socks, she was dressed in her standard summertime uniform: tee-shirt and shorts. The tee-shirt was courtesy of Harvey Bozzel's marketing campaign; this one had one of Quill's sketches of the Inn printed on the front.

Meg opened the door to the dairy Sub-Zero, peered in, and slammed it shut. She dragged a stool out from under the prep table and sat on it. "Your hair's a mess."

Quill poked vaguely at it. It was red, and there was a lot of it. "Maybe I should get it cut. I'll think about it after the wedding." She poured the beans into the grinder and added cold water to the well, wondering if she'd remembered to turn off her pot upstairs.

Meg stared glumly at the prep table counter top. "I mean, there is going to be a wedding. Right?"

"Are you taking coffee down to the fire?"

Quill looked doubtfully at the coffee pot, which was dripping merrily away. "I'd planned on it. Myles doesn't want me anywhere near the site, of course, but he'll like fresh coffee better. Meg, about the wedding . . ."

Meg blinked, as if to say, what wedding? She said,

"What did Myles tell you about the body?"

"Myles didn't say a word about a body. You were the one who told me about the body. That's because Andy told you. And to tell you the absolute truth, Meg, I don't want to think about bodies. Not today, not tomorrow, maybe not ever. We've had enough about bodies to last us a lifetime."

This indirect reference to the number of murder cases the two of them had been involved with in the past, brought a faint smile to Meg's face. Encouraged, Quill went on. "I wouldn't think that you'd want anything to do with bodies, either. Bodies and brides sound like a lousy mix to me."

Meg jumped off the stool and began a furious rummaging in the bread bin. "There's not a lot of breads left from last night, but for some reason the blueberry focaccia didn't go over that well. We can pack that up with the coffee."

"Don't you think we should at least talk about this?"

Meg cast a significant look at the kitchen clock. "It's practically five o'clock. In about ten minutes the first shift is going to show up and start baking croissants and brioche. And no, I don't want to get into a huge big hassle with you with fourteen prep chefs listening in."

"We only have two prep chefs," Quill said. "But I see your point."

"Bring your car to the back door, will you? I'll get this stuff packed up."

Quill sighed and went out the back door to pick up her Honda. The sky was lightening and the air was fresh and humid. She frowned a little at the skyline beyond the grove of trees where she had seen the false sunrise glow of the fire. The glow was gone, replaced by the mauve and pink of a real sunrise, but the scent of burning was stronger. She picked her way through the damp grass to the equipment shed, where she and Meg both kept their cars. Like everyone else in the Hemlock Falls, she kept her keys in the ignition. She backed out of the tool shed and bumped gently over the gravel to the back door. After a few moments, Meg edged her way out the kitchen door, a large thermos tucked under one arm and a stuffed paper bag in the other. She got into the front seat and balanced both parcels on her knees. "Have you seen Max?"

Quill looked around in a bewildered way for her dog. "Ever since John put that dog door in I don't know where he gets to half the time."

"That's because you leave the care of that dog totally up to me."

"What?" This was not true. This was also not the time to get into a stupid argument.

Meg scowled. "Are you going to sit here all day?" Quill bit her lip and counted backwards from ten. She put the Honda in reverse, backed up, and then headed down the drive. Meg jiggled her knees impatiently. "You're not taking the back roads to MacAvoy's place, are you?"

"The only way to get there is through back roads."

"They'll be clogged up with gawkers. If I were you . . ."

"You'd what, walk?" Quill said shortly.

"Max is down at the fire," Meg continued. "I'll bet you anything. And he's probably been run over by a fire truck by now . . . will you *watch* it, Quill? You almost clipped that corner. And put on your seat belt."

Quill put on her seat belt, which she hated because it made her feel like a baby in a high chair. She slowed down as they approached the scene of the fire. Meg was wrong about the congestion. Only six vehicles were pulled over in front of the smoldering pile of wood that had been MacAvoy's dilapidated barn: Myles' Jeep, Andy's Bronco, the Village's fire truck, the county ambulance, and a Ford pick-up she was pretty sure belonged to Mayor Elmer Henry. There was a black-and-white police cruiser, too, blocking the road. Deputy Davy Kiddermeister got out of the driver's seat as Quill pulled up. He was in full uniform and he was wearing his hat. Quill stopped the Honda and started to get out herself.

Davy waved and came toward them. "Sorry, Quill. Sheriff doesn't want anyone stopping. You'll have to go on back." He leaned forward. "Hi, Meg."

Meg scowled at him. "We've got coffee and a little food for everyone. How can Myles object to that?"

Davy's smooth pink face brightened. "Food from the Inn?"

"No, it's from Planet X. Just let us on through, David."

"Sorry, Meg. No civilians. Maybe you could leave the coffee and the food with me?"

"Maybe I couldn't." Meg levered herself out of the car and advanced purposefully toward the fire.

The barn had been small, as old barns go, and only two of the four walls had been upright. There was nothing left of it now, other than a damp, blackened pile of wet lumber. One of the yellow-coated firemen was rolling up the hose. Two more crouched in the ashes of the debris. Quill couldn't identify any of them. Near the ambulance, Myles towered over Andy Bishop's slighter form. Two men dressed in EMT whites rested against the rear doors of the ambulance. Max, the dog, poked around the ashes, his tail waving enthusiastically. A sour, stomach-churning odor hung in the air. There was very little smoke.

"I'm getting my dog out of there," Meg said. "Don't you dare try to stop me, or I'll report you to the ASPCA." She marched past Davy like a small, determined steam engine, the thermos bumping against her bare leg. Davy jogged after Meg. Myles turned to watch her, and from the set of his shoulders, Quill could tell Meg's visit was going to be of the shortest duration possible. From the set of Meg's shoulders, Quill could tell there was going to be an unholy argument, which, of course, her sister had been spoiling for. She got out of the Honda and stood for a moment, undecided about what to do. She could march after Meg and try to deflect the fight she was so determined to pick with her fiancé. On the other hand, she'd tried to change Meg's mind about creamed spinach, when Meg was two and Quill was six. Quill still suppressed an involuntary wince when presented with creamed spinach unexpectedly, and now she was thirty-six years old. Of course, she could just stand here, wait for the explosion, and then pick up the pieces.

A bright blue Lexus pulled up and parked behind the Honda and settled Quill's indecision for her. She waved a brief "hello" to Marge Schmidt and waited until Marge walked up and joined her.

"Burned that sucker right down to the ground," Marge said after a long moment spent observing the ruins. "Any idea how it started?"

"Hay?" Quill ventured. After more than ten years of living in a farming community, Quill knew the hazards of hay. Newly baled hay had a low combustion point, and more than one dairy farmer had lost hay barns to the resulting fires.

Marge snorted. "Not likely. Summer's been too dry."

Quill nodded wisely.

"Besides, MacAvoy hasn't used it for storage for years. Sucker didn't even have a roof."

Quill nodded again.

"Any hay that was in there," Marge went on, "is hay that would have been ten, fifteen years old." Marge rocked back on her heels and probed a molar with the tip of her tongue. Marge was short, sturdy, and on her off days, resembled nothing so much as a one-hundred-and-forty-pound Sherman tank. She had ginger-colored hair that curled around her bulletlike skull, and tiny, sharp blue eyes. She was probably the richest citizen in Tompkins County—but only Marge and her tax accountant knew for certain. She was certainly the best person at business within a one-hundred-and-fifty-mile radius, which included both Rochester and Syracuse, New York.

"Your company didn't insure the barn, did it?" Quill inquired sympathetically. Marge had recently added Schmidt Property and Casualty to her portfolio of successful businesses.

"Did. I don't anymore," Marge smiled in satisfaction. "That Maltby had some carrier from Rochester take it on after MacAvoy sold it off."

"Who's Maltby?"

Marge shrugged. "Some guy from downstate. Paid Bernie cash. Don't know what he wants it for. Zoning commission gave it a commercial license, but what kind of business are you gonna run out here? I offered a pretty good premium to insure the barn and land as is, but Maltby went somewhere else. Now who took that business from me?" She sucked her lower lip reflectively, her eyes on the activity at the site. The ambulance people looked as if they were ready to leave. The fire truck was packed and ready to go. "Got it." Her smile broadened. "Allied, I think it was. That little smarm Nussbaum. Too bad for Nussbaum. Bound to look bad for their loss ratio. Even a teeny little barn like this." Cheerfully, she unzipped her blue bowling jacket. The day was warming up, and it was going to be hot. "On the other hand," she added regretfully, "if it was arson, that's not going to affect Nussbaum one tiny little bit. Anybody say anything to you about arson?"

By anybody, Quill knew very well Marge meant Myles McHale. Her relationship to Myles was of keen interest to practically all the citizens of Hemlock Falls, especially since it tended to be on again, off again. It was the off-again parts that most interested Hemlockians. Nadine Nickerson, sole owner and proprietor of the Hemlock Falls Hall of Beauty told Quill it was better than *The Young and the Restless* any day of the week.

"Myles didn't say a word," Quill admitted. "But there hasn't been time to talk to him, Marge. I mean, we heard the alarm sound about four o'clock and he took off and that was, what, an hour and a half ago? I thought it'd take longer to get the fire out."

"Got that sucker doused pretty quick," Marge agreed. She shot Quill a keen sideways glance. "Myles say anything about a body?"

"No," Quill said truthfully. She had long ago ceased to be amazed at the speed with which information sped through Hemlock Falls. If she'd been a paranoid sort of person, she would have believed someone from the village had a permanent tap on her phone and a microphone in her living room wall. As it was, she asked, "How did you hear?"

"Bill Peterson was down to the diner for coffee when the ambulance call came in."

"I didn't realize you were open that early."

"Haying season," Marge said briefly, and Quill realized that, of course, during haying season farmers never seemed to get any sleep. For all she knew

Marge's diner was open twenty-four hours a day in August. "I see you and Meg brought something to take care of the boys."

Quill turned her attention back to the site of the fire. Meg was handing out Styrofoam cups of coffee. Andy stood with his arms folded, watching her. Davy Kiddermeister was scratching his head. Myles was engaged in deep conversation with one of the firemen.

Andy took a step forward. He said something—Quill and Marge were downwind, and Quill couldn't hear. "Oh, dear," Quill said involuntarily. Meg upended the thermos on the ground. She emptied the contents of the brown paper bag over Andy's head. Max leaped around them both, snapping at the cascade of breads and rolls that spilled out onto the grass. Meg finished up by throwing the thermos into the hedgerow to the left of the ash pile. Then she whirled and stamped back toward the car. Max dashed from the thermos to the spilled bread to the coffee cups and back again. Davy yelled at Max.

Marge folded her arms and leaned against the Honda's hood. Quill squeezed her eyes shut and opened them again. Max had confused Davy's pursuit with an invitation to play. He was engaged in that most aggravating of canine activates—dashing just out of arm's reach and barking loudly.

"That is the ugliest damn dog I ever did see," Marge observed. Quill, who was essentially a fair person, had to agree. Nobody knew for certain what Max's ancestry was, but it had to include standard poodle, Schnauzer, and what couldn't possibly be Giant Corgi, but must have been.

By now, Meg had trudged her way back to the Honda. Her face was red and her eyes were fierce. She took a deep breath and snapped, "Hi, Marge."

Marge nodded. "Meg. What's going on down there?"

"You would *think,*" Meg said with a furious glance over her left shoulder, "that I was the arsonist come back to view the scene of the crime. As to what's going on there, you can see for yourself. Three firemen, now leaving because the fire's out. One sheriff's deputy chasing Quill's dog . . ."

"How come he's *my* dog when he's being bratty?" Quill said indignantly.

". . . one totally unsympathetic sheriff and one bone-headed obnoxious bozo of a doctor."

Quill and Marge looked at each other, then looked away.

"Bride's nerves," Marge said in a surprisingly comfortable way. "Gin'll help, even though it's early for it. And you forgot the other bone-headed obnoxious bozo." She nodded at a second figure who'd been kicked off the site of the fire. "Here comes the mayor."

Mayor Elmer Henry, who seemed to get fatter every time Quill had run in to him this summer, bustled up breathlessly. "Quill, Marge." He nodded to each in turn, then mopped his forehead with the sleeve of his seersucker sports coat. He was probably in his mid-fifties, and the remains of his Southern boyhood could be heard in his speech, particularly when he was agitated.

Since Elmer found a lot to be agitated about, very few of his constituents failed to be reminded that he was a flatland foreigner. This didn't prevent him from being reelected every four years, which proved, Quill thought with affection, what an essentially nice place Hemlock Falls was.

"You got any news?" Marge asked.

Elmer's bluff face assumed a dignified expression. "I'm afraid I'm not at liberty to discuss that, Marge Schmidt. Not at liberty at all. As an elected official of this town, I nat'rally fall under the vows of secrecy incumbent upon the . . ."

"You don't know anything either," Marge said. "Shoot. Any idea of who the body is?"

Elmer sucked his lower lip nervously. "Nope. Don't know a thing about a body."

"Surely you must have seen the body," Quill said, surprised into speech. "I mean, my goodness, Elmer, why do you suppose the ambulance was there?"

"In case the firefighters got hurt, a' course."

Quill looked at Meg. Meg, lips compressed, was glaring at nothing in particular. Then she inhaled, testing the air. There had been a body. No question about it.

"When the cripes sake did you get here, Elmer?" Marge demanded. "If they took a body out of there, how come you didn't see it?"

"Just before Meg and Quill," Elmer said. "Adela woke me up around four on account of the alarm going off, but I thought it was just them kids over to the paint plant screwing around again. Then I got the phone call, a' course, so I came right over."

Marge's eyes narrowed. "What phone call? Who called you?"

Elmer was discomposed. "I dunno. Some guy." His lower lip pushed out. "Of course I'd get a phone call. As mayor of this town I had to get a phone call."

"That's odd," Quill said. "Was it an anonymous phone call?"

"No. Fella didn't tell me who it was, is all." Elmer looked from Quill to Meg and back again. "Body," he said with a shudder. Then, "Oh, glory. Not again. That's why you two are here, ain't it? To investigate another goldurned murder!"

CHAPTER 2

"So *is* it another goldurned murder?" Doreen Muxworthy-Stoker had bright black eyes and a halo of wild gray hair. When she was excited or interested she resembled an intelligent chicken. She set the clipboard containing the linen count down on the prep table and darted beady glances between her two employers, like a hen after corn.

"I don't know," Quill said. "The poor body was so badly burned they don't even know who it is yet."

"So what do they do, then? Like, send his teeth out for an ID? Something like that?"

Quill winced. Meg laughed. "Something like that, I guess," Quill said.

It was seven o'clock in the morning, and breakfast serving at the Inn was in full swing. Meg, Quill, and Doreen were drinking coffee in the kitchen, while the frantic activity of a gourmet kitchen at full capacity roiled around them. Bjarne Bjarnson, the designated master chef for this shift, swung tight-lipped around Meg, giving an occasional disapproving sniff when her eyes wandered in his direction. When he smacked down two plates of Eggs Quilliam so hard that he cracked the china, Meg had finally had it. She jumped off her stool and yelled, "What's wrong with you?!"

"I do not know what you mean." Bjarne said with dignity. "*Excuse* me." He brushed by her, dropped the eggs into the garbage can, plate and all, and stalked off in the direction of the Aga.

"I have every right to sit in my *own* kitchen."

"You are a bride," Bjarne said loftily. "You are supposed to be engaged in bridely things. Not snooping around to see if I am performing."

"Snooping!" Meg said. "Bull hockey."

"Bridely?" Quill said.

Bjarne put his hands on his hips and looked Meg straight in the eye. Since he was six-one and Meg was five-three, he had to bend over to do it. Which lessened the impressiveness of his performance. But not by much.

"I am in charge of this kitchen, am I not?" Bjarne said. "And when Jerry arrives . . ."

Meg threw her hands in the air. "Even *you* like Jerry Grimsby!"

". . . he will be maitre of dinners on Mondays, Wednesdays, and Fridays, and I will be in charge on Tuesdays, Thursdays, and Saturdays. This is Tuesday. I must ask you to leave my kitchen."

Meg gave him a long, level look. Then she reached for the eight-inch sauté pan. "You fat-headed Finn," she said sweetly.

"Yes, I am a Finn." Bjarne drew himself up. "And a man of honor. Were I about to be a bride, I would not be snooping around *you.*"

Quill reached out and enclosed Meg's hand in both of her own. "Meg? We have a few figures to go over in my office."

"What figures?"

"We got more' n that," Doreen said. "Not only do we got this murder to solve, but I want to talk to you, too."

"We don't know if it's a murder," Quill objected.

"Bullet hole right in the back of the head." Doreen said succinctly. "And that fire was set, or so I hear."

"Who'd you hear that from?" Meg asked. She'd apparently abandoned the notion of braining Bjarne.

Doreen shrugged. "Around. You know how it is."

Quill knew how it was in Hemlock Falls: Gossip, gossip, and more gossip. Still, there was usually a kernel of truth to even the wilder tales. She wasn't sure if this was because Hemlock Falls was a village of people who were essentially fair and reasonably kind, or if most Hemlockians were simply unimaginative and more literal-minded than the average. Whatever the reason, Doreen was probably right. It *was* murder.

"Hm," Meg said in an interested way.

"See? You don't have any time to stay here in the kitchen. There's a great deal to do today," Quill said.

"You shouldn't be bugging the heck of out Bjarne, anyways," Doreen interjected. "You act like you want him to quit. Try getting married without Bjarne here to lend a hand. You can just whistle for that wedding without Bjarne here."

Meg pursed her lips. "That's very true," she said thoughtfully. Her eyes wandered in the direction of the sauté pan.

Quill nudged Doreen with her elbow. "We've got those figures I mentioned *and* a murder to solve. Not to mention this week's schedule for the wedding."

"And me," Doreen said. "I need to sit down with you, too."

"Right," Quill said. "And we'll discuss whatever's on Doreen's mind. So, Meg. I'm calling a conference." She pulled Meg toward the swinging doors that led to the dining room. "Let's quit bugging Bjarne."

"I am *not* bugging Bjarne," Meg said coldly. "And come to think of it, it's the middle of the month. We don't do budgets and bills until the end of the month. So I don't know what figures you could be talking about. And we don't have any time to investigate this murder, Quill, you said so yourself. As for the wedding . . ." She grabbed the edge of the prep table. "Stop pulling me!"

"You *are* bugging me," Bjarne said. "You are bugging me very much." He folded his arms over his chest and gave Meg glare for glare. "Go away."

Doreen gave Meg a none-too-gentle push from behind. Quill drew her arm through Meg's. Together, they managed to drag Meg into the dining room. The hum and clatter of eighty-plus satisfied diners momentarily diverted Meg's attention. She followed Quill around the tables to the foyer, her eyes flicking over the contents of everyone's plate, muttering to herself.

Although most of Quill's concentration was on keeping Meg from picking up a salt cellar and flinging it back through the double doors to the kitchen, part of her mind was on the tables and the people sitting there. August was a prime month for lilies, and the sunny cream of the flowers accented the pale copper tablecloths in just the way that she'd planned. The sun flooded the floor-to-ceiling windows at an angle that filled the room with light, but didn't blind those guests seated near them. And as always, the sight of the falls beyond the long green lawn to the Gorge lifted her heart. It had been a hot, dry summer, and the water cascading over the limestone was half of its usual rush, but it was still beautiful. As they reached the foyer, Quill dropped her grasp on Meg's arm and went to the reception desk to check for messages.

Dina, the receptionist, came in at nine during the summer, and Mike had spent the early morning hours putting out the MacAvoy fire, so if any one had called (Myles, for example) they would have had to leave a message on the machine. The little light was blinking.

Meg dug her heels into the oriental carpet. "You are basically kidnapping me. You realize that, don't you?"

She made a one-hundred-and-eighty-degree turn and headed back to the kitchen. Doreen grabbed her by the back of the neck before she got farther than the maître d's desk.

"Now what's wrong?" Quill said. "I thought we'd decided to sit down in my office and make some plans."

"I have to go back there. Did you see the presentation on the Egg's Quilliam? Right there, at table seven. Darn it, Doreen. Let go!"

Quill grabbed the belt loop at the back of Meg's shorts. "You really should give Bjarne his chance," Quill said gently. "The poor guy's been looking forward to this for months. He's a good chef, isn't he? You can remember what it's like to want a chance."

Meg stopped struggling.

"He *could* be very, very good," she mumbled, "but he's a long way from very, very good. He's just very good."

"Push 'em out of the nest, I say," Doreen offered.

"Guy's gonna be very, very good, he's gotta fall on his keister some time, else how's he gonna learn anything?"

"By learning from me," Meg said icily. "That's how."

Quill opened the door to her office and pulled her sister through. "Sit down, shut up, and let me check the phone messages."

Meg threw herself on the office couch. It was covered in a fabric Quill particularly liked: chrysanthemums and cranes on a bronze background. Meg picked up a cinnamon chenille throw pillow and squashed it as flat as possible. Doreen settled herself on the edge of the wing chair with a scowl. That made two cranky people sitting on her couch. Quill sighed. The day was not starting well. "Well, Doreen. Here we are. What's the problem?"

Doreen sucked her lower lip reflectively. "Never had the time before to he'p you two with your cases."

"Why would you have any more time now than you've had before?" Meg asked crossly.

"Well, that's just the thing," Doreen said. "I wouldn't. But I would if I retired some."

Quill, her finger poised over the new calls button on the answering machine, forgot about the messages entirely and sat up in astonishment.

"You can't retire!" Meg said. "Good grief."

"Retire 'some'?" Quill said. "Retire *some?*"

Doreen coughed modestly. "Well, seein' as I have those shares in the company, I figured I'd be here for meetings and what not. Depending on where I'm at, of course."

A horrible suspicion flashed across Quill's mind. She looked at Doreen. She hadn't really looked at Doreen for weeks. You didn't spend every minute of every day examining the faces of people you loved for signs of a recurrence of breast cancer. You accepted the triumphant declaration of a cure with the kind of relief that made you faint, and then you went on with life.

Doreen gave Quill a bland, uninformative look.

"You're okay, aren't you?" Quill asked quietly.

"I'm finer than a frog hair," she said tartly.

Did she look fine? Did she look thinner? Doreen had settled into her seventies the way women who'd worked physically hard all their lives often did. Her hands were broad, gnarled with arthritis. Her shoulders were bent and she walked like a sailor, rocking slightly from side to side. She was thin—but not, surely, with the cadaverous thinness of cancer? She'd always been wiry and her skin was wrinkled from a lifetime of hours spent outdoors gardening, hanging clothes out to dry, and just walking from her house in the village to the Inn every day of the year. "I figured this might be a good time to bring this up, what with all the changes goin' on around here. This is just another little change. You won't even notice it."

It was the worst possible time to bring this up. Quill sank into the chair behind her desk. If Andy knew anything, he wouldn't tell her; she knew that from past experience. He was remorselessly ethical. Besides, Doreen's mastectomy had been done in Syracuse. There was no way the physicians there would talk to her. Stoke? Could she talk to Doreen's husband?

"Now's a good time to bring this up?" Meg said doubtfully.

"Well, it's a good time for me," Doreen said candidly. "Thing is, I was figuring you might promote that Kathleen to housekeeper. She's got a good head on her shoulders, and I know for a fact she'd like the promotion."

"Good waitresses earn as much in seasonal tips as the

housekeeping job pays in a year," Quill said. "And she'd have to work all year round."

"She puts in a seventy-hour week in season," Doreen said. "And it ain't the cash, so much. Heck, if it'd been the cash, I woulda ditched bossin' around them maids for waitressing years ago."

Quill pinched her lip, hard. Doreen's standards of acceptable guest behavior were high. She expressed her displeasure with a judicious application of the dust mop. She didn't even want to think of an aggravated Doreen with a plate of hot soup at the ready. "Too many lethal weapons available in the dining room. Most of your career as a waitress would have been spent in county justice court."

Doreen grinned. "Maybe so. But you got your medical, your pension, and your insurance with this housekeeping job. Kathleen's got those three kids and a no-good husband. And there's a couple of trips Stoke and me want to take. And of course, there's this here murder. You two are gonna need some help with that. And I was thinking maybe you could find something else around here for me to do."

Quill took a deep breath. "Trips," she said. "And murder, huh? Well." She ran her hands through her hair and rubbed the back of her neck. Stoke wouldn't tell her a thing, not without Doreen's permission. And Doreen would tell her when she was ready. But she was going to worry herself to death if she didn't find out what was really going on with her housekeeper—or what now appeared to be her former housekeeper. "You're not just going to take off and leave us right this minute, are you?" she said.

Meg snorted. "Good grief, Quill. You sound absolutely pathetic."

"I don't know if you realize it or not," Quill said stiffly. "But Doreen just quit! And it's probably because—you know. It's back."

"What are you talking about?!" Doreen scolded. "Nothin's back!" She opened her eyes in alarm. "You firin' me?"

"Of course I'm not firing you!"

"Quill, Quill, Quill." Meg shook her head. "She said she wanted to retire 'some.' That's what you said, Doreen, right? That you wanted to retire 'some.' "

"That's right. Tell you the truth, I'm getting bored cleaning rooms."

"See? She didn't just quit." Meg bounced the throw pillow on her knees. "She wants to spend some time with Stoke. She wants to explore new challenges." She gave Doreen an I-understand-Quill's-reaction-perfectly smile. "You know what's going on here, don't you? I mean, Quill's overreaction to a perfectly natural request and going allover nutso."

"I did *not* go allover nutso."

"You have to keep these things in proportion, Quill."

Quill gritted her teeth.

"What?" Doreen asked suspiciously. "What's going on here?"

"She's having a panic attack. Because of her lack of proportion, of course."

"What's all that about when it's at home?"

"I am not having a panic attack," Quill said. "And my sense of proportion's just fine, thank you very much."

"Of course you're having a panic attack. You're thinking that with me out of the kitchen and Doreen out of the housekeeping, and John with his consulting business in Syracuse you're going to have to run the Inn all by yourself."

Quill grabbed the curls over her ears and pulled them hard. It didn't help. She wanted to scream anyway. "Meg, you are *not* out of the kitchen."

"You're darn right, I'm not. I'll just have to tell Andy's the wedding's off."

Quill put her head on her desk and banged it gently against the desk blotter.

"Temporarily, of course," Meg said sunnily. "We'll reschedule it around Thanksgiving, or maybe Christmastime."

The phone rang. Quill stared at it. For the hundredth time, she wished she had one of those little gizmos that told you who was calling. Meg was shaking her head and mouthing "I'm not here if it's Andy." Doreen had begun an it's-time-you-stopped-jerking-that-Andy-around tirade, which Quill had heard before and which got louder and louder as Doreen got madder and madder. Whoever was on the line was going to think they'd called an asylum and not a professionally run three-star establishment capable of handling any crisis, large or small.

Maybe she should let the answering machine kick in.

"Will you just answer the damn thing?" Meg shrieked. "And Doreen, just cool it!"

Quill picked the phone up and said, "The Inn at Hemlock Falls, may I help you?" with a heavy Southern accent, just in case.

"Uh," Elmer Henry said. "Uh. I think I maybe got . . . no, you said it's the Hemlock Inn, didn't ya? I'd like to speak to Miss Sarah Quilliam, please. And say," he added in a chatty, confiding way, "where ya from?"

Quill removed the receiver from her ear, looked at it, then said, "One moment please," and jiggled the receiver. She said, "Hello? Hello? Hello?" and hung up.

Surprised into silence, both Meg and Doreen stared at her. The phone shrilled again.

"Not. One. Word," Quill said. She picked up and said, "Hello? Sarah Quilliam. May I help you?"

"That you, Quill?"

"It is, Elmer."

"You count your guests this morning?"

Quill bit back her immediate response, which was "What do you think this is, a Gulag?" and said, "not this morning, no."

Elmer must have put his hand over the receiver; she heard a muffled mutter, then he came back on the line. "Marge and I were chewing this over, here."

"Chewing what over? Where are you?"

"At the diner. We were talking about this here murder. Figured you and Meg might not mind a little help on this one." He chuckled. Quill imagined the expression on Myles' face when he realized that what seemed to be the entire village of Hemlock Falls was anxious to give its two amateur detectives a hand in solving a rumored murder. She didn't have to imagine the expression on his face when he realized she and Meg probably were going to investigate this murder. She'd seen it before.

"Thing is, we're not missing anybody here, down to the diner. Thought if you two were missing a guest, we could start there."

"Actually, that's not a bad idea," Quill said, because it wasn't. And if she sent Meg off to count heads, it might divert her volatile sister's current desire to smash all the wedding plans to smithereens. "We'll check it out." She glanced at her sister, who had subsided into a blue funk on the sofa. Doreen had subsided into a blue funk, too, although why, Quill couldn't imagine. "Meg will call you back. Will you be at the diner very much longer?"

"I got to meet a fella about some bidness here, first." Elmer said importantly. "Don't know how long that's going to take. Why don't you report to me at the Chamber meeting at ten this morning. Get there a little early, 'kay? And don't forget the Resort Gala meeting this afternoon, Quill. You can't be late to that one."

Quill suppressed a groan. Elmer hung up before she could tell him that she wouldn't be able to make either the Chamber meeting or be on the Resort Gala Committee because she was going to be stark staring crazy in about five minutes, and by ten o'clock little guys in white jackets would have hauled her off to a place without weddings, resignations, grouchy Finns, and village officials with detectival delusions.

She reflected a long moment on her own detectival delusions. "Hey, guys," she said cheerfully. "Elmer had a good idea. Did you notice if all our guests were here this morning?"

"I haven't the faintest idea who's here." Meg said glumly. "Why?"

Quill explained.

"Well, Dina would know. She checks everybody in and everybody out. Ask her."

"Good idea."

Quill picked up a pencil and fiddled with it. Doreen and Meg stared at her. She opened her mouth to suggest that they each get started with their day before she realized that neither of them had a day to start. Doreen had just quit. Meg had agreed not to go near the kitchen. And if she went near Andy again, they could kiss all the wedding plans goodbye since Meg wanted to pound him flatter than a filet. She cleared her throat. "Okay, guys, Here's a suggestion. Doreen could you talk to Kathleen about the promotion? And then you can start filling her in and what she's going to need to do. John's in town this week, so perhaps you could stop by his office and see what kind of paperwork we'll need to get underway. And you might ask Kathleen who she'd pick to take her place scheduling the waitstaff. Peter Hairston might be a good choice, if she agrees. And Meg . . ." She trailed off. Her sister looked woefully at her. "Why don't you bring some of your things back to your old rooms? Just for a few days," she added hastily.

"Until the wed—until whatever. And would you want to spend the afternoon at the Croh Bar picking up clues?"

For years, the Croh Bar had been the closest thing to a dive within forty miles of Hemlock Falls. Marge and her business partner, Betty Hall, had taken it over several years ago. It was still a bar, but it was, as Betty Hall claimed, a diner bar. Everybody in Hemlock Falls spent a lot of time there, drinking coffee and eating Betty's great food in the mornings, and drinking beer and eating Betty's great food in the afternoons.

Meg shook her head. "You want me to spend the afternoon getting pie-eyed?"

"I think you should spend the afternoon detecting," Quill said. "There's no better place to pick up what's going on. They'll know the identity of the body in the barn before Myles and Davy do."

Meg smiled, a little. The smile twisted. "It's very weird," she said abruptly. "I don't know what to do with my days." She blinked away tears. "Do you realize what a horrible feeling that is? I can tell you just what's going to happen after I get married. Jerry Grimsby will take over the kitchen by popular acclaim, I'll be waiting at home while Andy's latest emergency bats her foot-long eyelashes at him when he's covering the ER and I'll get fat!"

Quill didn't mention panic attacks of any proportion although she really wanted to. She didn't use the word "nutso," either.

"So I'll go sit at the Croh Bar and get soused!" Meg

said tragically. "Chatting people up!"

Quill, who would have been perfectly happy sitting with a sketchbook at the Croh Bar for weeks at a time and letting the rest of the world, except for Myles, go hang, tried as hard as she could to imagine panic over nothing to do, and failed. "Yes, well, chatting people up is an important way to spend the day, in my opinion. We don't spend half as much time chatting people up as we should. It isn't just the murder, Meg. There's a lot of town business that just whips by and takes us by surprise."

"Such as?"

"The resort for example. It's due to open in two weeks, and there's a whole big hoopla around that. I mean, not just what the Chamber's doing for it, which is minor stuff, really, but other stuff."

"Like what?" Meg said skeptically.

Quill waved her arms. "I'll know more when I go to the Resort Gala Committee meeting this afternoon. The governor's coming to the opening ceremonies, right? Maybe somebody knows somebody who can talk him into staying overnight in Hemlock Falls. Maybe he could stay here! There's a lot of stuff happening around the resort opening. Talk to people. Keep your ear to the ground." Quill was warming herself up to this, she could feel it. "Look, here's something for both of you. Really, Doreen, you could do this part-time, too. After the Golden Pillars Group leaves here this afternoon, we've got three suites open and no bookings for them until November. So you both have a couple of significant things to do this afternoon. Check around for anything possibly suspicious about this murder. And see if there's anyone we can book to stay at the Inn. Especially while the opening ceremonies for the resort are going on, although I bet you guys can come up with some other ideas. Then tonight we can go out to dinner, just the three of us, and talk about it. You know what!" Quill leaned forward, "We can go out to somebody else's restaurant!"

Meg sat up a little straighter and stopped mangling the throw pillow. Doreen went "hm" in a pleased way.

"Whoa," Meg said thoughtfully. "We haven't checked out the competition for years. What about Elise's in Ithaca?"

Quill sat back. "Perfect. Wherever you want to go is fine with me."

"I could dress up, some," Doreen said. "Stoke bought me a black pantsuit as a present, after the doctor."

"That was so nice of him," Quill said warmly. Then, mildly, "Which doctor?"

Doreen screwed up her face. "I s'pose it's better than some things."

"What's better?" Quill asked.

"Arthritis." Doreen held out both hands in front of her. "Osteo-whatis. Here. In my legs, too. I don't know. It's a load of baloney, far as I can see. I feel fine."

"And the doctor said you should take it easy for a while?" Quill said. "My goodness, Doreen. Is that it?"

Meg touched Doreen's hands lightly, said, "I'm so glad it's nothing else!" and burst into tears.

Doreen groped in her apron pocket and pulled out a wad of Kleenex. Quill poured Meg a glass of water and made her take an aspirin. Doreen patted Meg's back until Meg gulped, scrubbed at her face with both fists and yelled, "I'm fine!"

"Good," Quill said. "So what do you think? Croh Bar? New business?"

"I'll find us somebody good." Doreen got to her feet with a grin. "Travel agent. Sounds like a good career to me. You do a lot of sittin' in a travel agency. You might think about that, Meg, if you want to get out of the food business."

"I don't want to get out of the food business." Meg's eyes narrowed thoughtfully. "I've got something in mind already." She rose abruptly. "All right. Look, I'm going to pick up some things from Andy's, okay? It's pretty clear you need me back here for a while. I'll leave him a note or something. We'll meet at what—five-thirty? That'll give us enough time to change and drive into Ithaca. And Quill—I'm not making any reservations at the restaurant, okay? We're just going to show up and see how they handle it."

"How who handles what?" Quill said, bewildered.

Meg smiled. It wasn't a smile Quill entirely trusted. She'd seen it before. "And I'll get to the Croh Bar if I can, but I've got a couple of errands to run in Syracuse first." She slammed out of the office with something of her old enthusiasm. Quill tugged thoughtfully at her lower lip.

"Well!" Doreen slapped both knees and got to her feet

with a groan. "I'll go hunt up that Kathleen."

"Just a minute." Quill said.

Doreen gave her a look. It was a don't-even-start-with-me look. She hated concern, which she called "sticking your nose in." The only nose Doreen approved of sticking in anyone's business was her own.

"I don't know what the heck you're going on about," Doreen said, although Quill hadn't said a word. She banged out of the door after Meg and narrowly missed careening into Dina, who jumped agilely aside, and without missing a beat said, "Bye' Doreen. Hey, Quill. Can we talk about something for a minute?"

"Hey, Dina." Quill looked at the clock on her desk. "It's only nine o'clock? I've got the whole rest of the day to get through?"

"Well, twenty after." Dina said conscientiously. "I would have been here right smack on time, Quill, if it weren't for Max."

Quill looked around, as if expecting to see her dog curled up in his usual spot by the filing cabinet. She recalled the last time she'd seen him, poking around the remains of the fire. "Where is Max?"

"Well, that's just it. Davy's like, you know, a hyper spaz, which I suppose he has a right to be, but honestly Quill, if you'd just trained that dog better, life would be a lot easier for everybody. I," she continued, with a virtuous air, "tried my best to catch him, but it was no-way-Jose." She pushed her round, red-rimmed glasses back up on her nose and regarded Quill with a great deal of injured innocence.

"Where is he?"

"Messing around in those woods by the MacAvoy murder."

"It was Mr. MacAvoy that was murdered?" Quill said, dismayed. "Oh, no. He was a sweet little guy. Who would want to murder Bernie MacAvoy?"

Dina shrugged. "I didn't know it was Mr. MacAvoy who was murdered."

"But you just said . . ."

"What I said was Max ran off with something from the burned-down barn and Davy's fit to be tied. It's too bad Myles went off to the forensics lab in Syracuse. Max always comes when Myles calls him."

"You didn't say that at all," Quill pointed out. "Gosh, Dina. What did he run off with? Not . . ." Quill grimaced and despite herself, she lowered her voice, "not a bone or anything like that?"

"Wow," Dina said soberly. "I, like, didn't think about that at all. All Davy said was that it was a vital piece of evidence. A bone would be a vital piece of evidence, wouldn't it? I mean, not a toe bone, or a finger bone, but a skull or the poor guy's teeth . . ."

"Stop," Quill said. She glanced at the clock again. "Shoot. I've got a Chamber meeting in half an hour. The woods in back of the vegetable gardens, you said? The ones that surround the MacAvoy farm on the far side? Okay, I'll take the Honda."

"And some roast beef," Dina suggested. "Or I could give you one of my fruit wraps. He likes raspberry."

"He hates raspberry," Quill said, remembering the

stains on the oriental carpet in the foyer. "But the roast beef's a good idea." She gathered up her purse and her car keys. "Dina. The mayor had a good idea."

"Mayor Henry?" Dina said skeptically.

"About that poor corpse. Are we . . ." Quill hesitated, searching for a more tactful phrase than, "missing any guests."

"Is everybody who's registered here, here?"

Dina blinked at her. Her eyes were large and brown, and she was a pretty girl with an open expression. Most people were slightly taken aback when they learned she was a PhD candidate in limnology at nearby Cornell University. "You mean like, as opposed to the Marriott out on Route Fifteen?"

"No, I mean as opposed to lying under the remains of Bernie MacAvoy's barn."

"Well, whoever it is would be at the forensics lab in Syracuse with Myles," Dina said, with her usual regard for the literal, "but I see what you mean. Hm. No. And I can't think of anyone who would be murderable, if you see what I mean."

"No, I don't," Quill said tartly. "What in the world does that mean?"

"Well, all the married couples we have seem to be very happy, except for Meg and Andy of course, and they aren't even marri—"

"Stop."

"Sorry." Dina stared at the carpet, frowning. "Wait! Oh! Of course. The sleazolas."

"The what?"

"They checked in late yesterday and went right out again. You haven't met them yet. Rooms 311 and 226. From Rochester. Leo 'Boom-Boom' Maltby and his business partner, let's see . . . Norwood Ferguson. The business is Lovejoy Enterprises."

"What makes you call them sleazolas?" Quill said. "Honestly, Dina. You should really work on this business of being polite to the guests. And I know very well who they are. I booked their reservation myself. I just haven't met them yet. They're supposed to be giving a presentation to the Chamber this morning at ten."

"Well, you won't forget them when you do," Dina said, unfazed. "One's short and dark and hairy and the other one's tall, fat, and bald and it's not the nice kind of fat, either. It's wiggly. They both smoke these perfectly revolting cigars and the short one," Dina stopped for a breath then continued, unperturbed. "The short one pinched my boobs."

"You're not serious."

"I am perfectly serious. Stuck a big fat cigar in his teeth, pulled out this whacking big gold cigar lighter, lit it, snapped it shut, leaned over the reception desk and said, 'No silicone there, Norrie. Betcha a ten spot.' And then, *pinch!*"

"Good grief. Why didn't you call Mike to throw him out?"

"Oh, I don't know," Dina said. "He was a sleazola, but he was a cheerful sleazola, if you get my drift."

"You know our policy on that kind of thing, Dina. I'm so sorry. I wish you'd said something."

“You want me to say something, I’ll say it now: It’s nine-forty-five and you’d better get going if you’re going to find Max before the meeting. Tell you what, when good old Maltby gets up to give his speech or whatever you can, like, give him an icy stare.”

“I’ll give him a right hook, if you like,” Quill said determinedly. “We’ll talk about this when I get back.”

“But . . .”

Quill sat back down. “Is there something else?”

“I was, like, thinking about getting another job.”

“Another job?”

Dina took her glasses off. She looked very young. “Something a little more glamorous.”

“Glamorous?”

“Do you know how long I’ve been in graduate school?”

“I know it must seem like a long time, yes.”

“I think I’m burned out. I, like, really need a change, Quill.”

“Is it the copepods?” Dina’s doctoral thesis had something to do with the lifecycle of this small, amoebalike creature.

“Not really. It just seems that life is passing right by me. You know? And I spend half my life in green waders. They are so ugly.”

“I know.” Quill tried not to look at the clock. “I’ve got a great idea. Why don’t you join Doreen and Meg and me for dinner tonight? I’m taking everybody to Elise’s. All of us need a break. It’ll be a girl’s night out. And we can talk about it then. Right now . . .”

Dina nodded. "You've got to find Max and that finger bone."

Quill got to the kitchen in record time, grabbed a slice of raw beef from the meat Sub-Zero and raced out of the back door. It was, she saw, an absolutely beautiful day. It was hot, as it always was in August in upstate New York, but the humidity was low. The scent of roses mingled with the heavy perfume of the oriental lilies. Behind her, she could hear the rush of the falls. She suddenly felt warmly toward Max. It might take a very long time to find her dog, she thought cheerfully. Maybe the entire length of the Chamber meeting. She pursed her lips in what she knew would be a hopeless "come here!" whistle, and called, "Max? Here boy."

Of course her dependably undependable dog showed up immediately.

And he dropped a twenty-four-carat-gold cigar lighter at her feet.

CHAPTER 3

The cigar lighter was inscribed in one of those curly fonts that Quill particularly disliked. She wiped the dog slobber off it and read: BOOM BOOM BOOM! ALWAYS S.

Max barked, rolled vigorously in the grass, then sat up looking proud of himself.

Quill didn't know where Max had come from before he strolled into their lives four years ago, but she was pretty sure that his former owner had encouraged him to leave, and not at all kindly. Even raised voices made Max scramble backwards, head down, ears flattened against his lumpy skull. So with patient affection, she scratched him under his chin and said, "You are a bad, bad dog, to swipe evidence, Max." Then she gave him the beef.

"*Now* what do I do?"

Max licked the remains of the beef from his jaws, sniffed at her hopefully, realized immediately she was beef-free, then sat back and looked at her in a very intelligent way.

"I absolutely have to call Myles, of course." She patted the pocket of her skirt for her cell phone, squinted at the tiny display window and punched the key that was supposed to dial Myles direct. She got his voice mail, which meant he was in a meeting somewhere, because Myles always kept his cell phone on, and she left a conscientiously accurate message. "It's me. Max retrieved a gold cigar lighter that's about four-inches long and an inch-and-a-half in diameter," (Quill was very good at measurements) "and inscribed, 'Boom Boom Boom Always S.' It's 24 carat," (Quill was good at metals, too) "and really, really vulgar." She paused a moment. This was an opinion, not a fact, and Myles was forever reminding her there was very little room for speculation and opinion in forensics because the other side could always argue it wasn't so. "Strike the part about it being vulgar. And Dina told me one of the guests here, a Leo Maltby, used a big gold cigar lighter to light his cigar before he pinched her in a highly inappropriate way. And no one's seen him since." She cleared her throat and added, diffidently, "It looks as if he might be the victim, Myles. I thought you'd want the forensics guys in Syracuse to know." She added modestly, "Just luck on my part," and punched the end button.

She was half-way down the hall to the Conference Room for the Chamber meeting when her cell phone rang. Actually, it didn't ring. It played the first few bars of "Rondo Alla Turco." Dina had programmed the phone when John Raintree first bought it for her, and Quill didn't know how to make it stop. "Rondo Alla Turco" was hummable. The last time her phone rang in public, she was at the CVS drugstore buying shampoo and the guy next to her hummed along with it all the way to the check out counter.

Quill punched the end button by mistake, punched the missed calls button and eventually got Myles.

"Hey," she said. "Did you get my message?"

"I did." Myles paused, and asked, "You said you haven't seen him since. Since when?"

"Well, I actually didn't see him at all," Quill said. "I was in Ithaca with Meg all day yesterday for her dress fitting and they checked in and went out right away, Dina said." She backed up against the wall to let Miriam Doncaster and Howie Murchinson get by to go to the Conference Room.

"He checked in with someone else?"

"Norwood somebody," Quill said a little guiltily. Archie Godwin would have remembered Maltby's roommate's name. "Dina should know. How's it going at your end?"

Myles didn't answer this. Instead he said, "I may be late tonight," told her he loved her, reminded her she was not a member of any law enforcement agency in the state of New York or any other venue, and said goodbye.

And not one word of thanks for her brilliant discovery of the name of the murder victim.

She followed Miriam and Howie to the end of the hall and stopped outside the Conference Room door. The room was long and narrow. An oversize mahogany table filled almost the whole of the space. At least twenty of the thirty chairs available were crowded with members of the Hemlock Falls Chamber of Commerce, all of them chattering like Canadian geese on a pond. The mayor was pacing up and down in front of the whiteboards at the opposite end. Quill smiled at everyone in a general sort of way and sat at the farthest end, between Miriam and Marge Schmidt. This impeded her view of the mayor, who sat at the head of the table, which was just as well, since she'd forgotten to bring the minutes from the last meeting.

Elmer whacked the gavel on the table. It took several tries before the room settled into a semblance of quiet. "Okay, now. We got a lot of stuff to get through this morning. Rev'run, you wanna do the prayer? A short one, if you don't mind."

Dookie Shuttleworth, minister of the Hemlock Falls Church of the Word of God, rose to his feet with his sweet, absented-minded smile. His wispy hair floated around his face like the last gasp of a dandelion. He clasped his hands, said "Bless us all!" in a very surprised way and sat down again.

"Right," Elmer said hurriedly. " 'Kay. I'm gonna dispense with the minutes from our last meeting." He whacked the gavel again. "Minutes accepted. Now, we got any old bidness? Nope, no old bidness." Whack! "Okay, new bidness. 'Fraid to tell you all that our presentation for this morning has been cancelled. So, unless somebody's got something to say, I move we adjourn." He swung the gavel up to whack it a final time. Harland Peterson extended a work-calloused hand and arrested the gavel in mid-air. "Hang on there, Elmer. You're in some kind of hurry. And you're sweating up a storm. What you up to, anyways?"

Quill peered around Marge's bulk. Marge had ditched her bowling jacket in the morning warmth, and Quill saw that she was wearing a bright red tee-shirt that read SCHMIDT! AND HALL! ALL-AMERICAN DINER! FINE FOOD! AND FAST! in large bronze letters. Harvey Bozzel had been busy. And Elmer did look nervous, now that Quill took a moment to really look at him. It was warm in the conference room, despite the air conditioning, but that didn't explain the sweat beading the mayor's broad pink brow.

"No rush, Harland. Just tryin' to be efficient. We all have a lot to do today. Thought we'd get this meeting over with as quick as we can so folks can get out and get some work done. And since, like I said, the presentation's been cancelled, we don't have a whole lot to cover." He tried unsuccessfully to wrest the gavel from Harland's hand.

Harland frowned. He was a big man in his early sixties, and the largest dairy farmer in Tompkins County. Years of hard work in the fields and barns had weathered both his skin and his sensitivity to the texture of a saddle. He plucked the gavel from Elmer's hand and stuck it handle down in the breast pocket of the mayor's seersucker jacket. "What we got to do this morning is listen to that Maltby and his plans for MacAvoy's old barn. Some reason you don't want us to hear what Maltby's got to say?"

"I don't have the least idea of what Maltby's gonna tell us," Elmer blustered. "But when a guy's supposed to show up for a ten o'clock meeting of the Chamber of Commerce in this town, well, he'd just better show up at ten o'clock, that's all. And he ain't here, and I haven't got any calls telling me why he ain't here so I'm canceling it."

Quill fingered the gold cigar lighter in her pocket. "Actually," she said apologetically, "I don't think we can expect to see Mr. Maltby anytime soon."

Marge turned and eyed her sharply. Actually, everyone in the room narrowed their eyes at her. Quill felt like the hunted deer with the target birthmark on his chest in the infamous Gary Larson cartoon.

"What d'ya mean, 'anytime soon'?" Marge demanded. "You and that sister of yours know something about the body in the barn?"

Esther West (she wore a button that read WEST'S BEST DRESS SHOPPE!—Harvey was diversifying) leaned past Marge and hissed, "I heard it was Mr. MacAvoy himself they found in there, Quill." She leaned back in her seat and patted the spit curls over her left ear. " 'Course, I called up his daughter to see if she might want to come in and look at the new fall line—black's back, Quill, by the way—and I didn't get an answer!"

Marge gave a rude snort. "MacAvoy was down to the diner this morning, Esther. Talking a mile a minute to the mayor there. So he ain't dead, not by a long shot. And whatever Elmer was hearing from MacAvoy, he didn't like at all." She turned her turret-like gaze on the mayor and pursed her lips in thought.

Esther breathed peppermint in Quill's direction. "So? Myles told you who was murdered?"

"Myles didn't, no." Quill smiled modestly. "I'm afraid I can't say anything more than that."

"More than what?!" Esther said indignantly. "You haven't said a word. Are you and Meg on the case? You can tell me that at least."

"Meg's getting married in three days," Marge said. "She doesn't have time to go chasing murderers."

"That's not what I heard," Esther said. "I heard that Meg dumped a whole pot of coffee over poor Dr. Bishop's head and that the wedding's off." She shook her head. "Poor, poor Andy. I know she's your sister. Quill, but honestly, she's led that man a merry chase."

Fortunately for Esther, Quill became aware that someone was shouting her name.

"Quill!" Harland shouted, in the rising tones of someone who's called out more than once.

"Yes, sorry. Is the meeting over?" Quill rose to her feet.

"We wanted to know how come we're not gonna be seeing Maltby."

Elmer shrugged, "Guy's left town, probably. No harm in that."

"Quill knows something we don't know," Miriam Doncaster said. The town librarian tugged imperatively at Quill's sleeve. "C'mon. Was it Mr. Maltby in that fire?"

"More than likely," Quill said coolly. "More than that I can't say at this juncture. But I will ask if anyone here recognizes this." She pulled the cigar lighter from her skirt pocket and held it up.

A fat, hairy hand snaked around her left shoulder and snatched the cigar lighter. "Hey! I wondered where that got to."

Quill turned around in surprise. Two men stared at her. One was short and hairy. The other was shaped like the Pillsbury Doughboy, only much taller. Both of them wore gold chains around their necks, white patent-leather loafers, and extremely colorful Hawaiian shirts. The tall one had a roll of blueprints under one arm.

The short hairy one held an unlit cigar in his right hand and the gold cigar lighter in the other. He waved genially at the crowd. "Ladies. Gents."

"Who in the world are you?" Quill said. Then she felt herself blush. "I'm sorry. I didn't mean to be rude."

"Leo Maltby," he said with a hospitable grin. He had very white, very large teeth.

"You're not!" Quill blurted. "You can't be. You're dead."

Maltby rolled his eyes. "Do I look dead, dolly?"

His partner whirled his forefinger around his left ear. "Pitiful, innit?" he observed. "She's a looker, too."

Maltby's eyes drifted downward to her chest. Quill crossed her arms defensively. His gaze shifted beyond Quill to the front of the room, where Elmer stood with a panicky look on his face. "This the Chamber of Commerce meeting, right? Yo, Mayor. You want to introduce us, or you just gonna stand there with your teeth in your mouth?"

Elmer frowned and shuffled papers.

"No? You're just gonna stand there. Right. Well, grab yourself by the shorthairs and keep your powder dry. I'll be right up." Leo edged his way past the chairs and down the length of the room. He clapped the men on their shoulders and grinned at the women. A strong odor of L'Homme drifted in his wake.

Belatedly, Quill recalled his partner's name: Norwood Ferguson. With a vague sense she'd been inhospitable, she turned to say hello.

Ferguson had already clumped around to the other side of the table and was working his way to the mayor with all the enthusiasm of Eeyore predicting the weather. The blueprints under his arm smacked Nadine Peterson and Esther West on the head as he went by. Both men reached the head of the table at the same time. Ferguson slumped against the whiteboard, stood the blueprints against the wall, and assumed the air of a spectator. Maltby leaned forward, clamped his cigar in his mouth, and splayed his knuckles on the polished mahogany table. He swept the table with an appreciative leer. "I just wanna tell ya, the ball and chain just about wet her pants when she first saw this place. This Hemlock Falls is a beaut! And it's her you got to thank for the plans me and Norrie here got for you."

"Ball and chain?" Miriam Doncaster said, in the kind of voice that iced warm drinks.

"What plans?" Harland Peterson said. "You bought MacAvoy's old barn, didn't you?"

"You planning to sue somebody on account of the old barn burned down?" Marge asked, with an air of spurious concern. "Allied's got that policy. Guy named Nussbaum. I got his number if you want it."

"Who *is* this person, Elmer?" This from Adela Henry, the mayor's formidable wife. She gazed at Maltby in horror.

Howie Murchinson cleared his throat. "We might let the man speak," he suggested. As the least-litigious lawyer in town—and the Justice of the Peace—he carried the kind of social authority that Elmer has always aspired to. He folded his arms, leaned back in his chair, and peered judiciously at Maltby over his wire-rimmed spectacles. "Mr. Maltby? You have the floor."

"Standing on it, isn't he?" Ferguson said with a chuckle.

"Shut up, Norrie," Maltby said in a kindly way. "Pin

those drawings up, will ya?" He redirected his attention to the crowd. "These are the plans for that old barn we bought last week. Got the zoning approval set yesterday, figured we should let you people know what's going down."

Ferguson unrolled the blueprints. But they weren't blueprints at all, but a very large pad of paper bound at the top and with a large hook in the middle. Ferguson hung the pad in the center of the whiteboard. The cover sheet was bright pink with huge neon-green letters that read:

LOVEJOY'S NUDIE BAR AND GRILL
50 ALL-NAKED WOMEN 50

"And we're going to hire every one of our new employees from right here in Hemlock Falls," Leo Maltby said proudly. "Don't anyone complain to *me* about unemployment."

CHAPTER 4

The first thing Quill did after the Chamber of Commerce meeting was march into the Tavern Lounge and ask Nate the bartender for one ounce of very cold Grey Goose vodka. She drank it thoughtfully. The second thing she did was to call Myles, whose cell phone was off, thank goodness, to tell him that his corpse wasn't Leo "Boom-Boom" Maltby. Although, she'd added, aware of a sense of injustice at the current turn of events, Mr. Maltby might be a corpse pretty soon if Miriam Doncaster and the Ladies Fireman's Auxiliary had anything to say about it. The third was to try and leave the Inn for the day by way of the french doors at the end of the Lounge before half of the Chamber, infuriated by the plans for Lovejoy's Nudie Bar and Grill, found her and forced her to join another committee.

She was too late. Just as she reached the doors to the outside terrace, Miriam marched into the Lounge. "There you are!" she shrieked. The Tavern Lounge was full, but her voice carried over the hum of conversation like Custer's bugle.

Quill let the french door swing shut and remained inside. Miriam marched across the polished oak floor like Cotton Mather on a search for sinners, attracting interested glances, if no potential converts. She was followed by Adela Henry (shell-shocked), Esther West (appalled, in a pleased way), and Carol Anne Spinoza. Carol Anne, Hemlock's meanest (and only) tax assessor, looked gob-smacked.

"You shot out of that meeting before we could talk." Miriam complained. "We've got to do something about this, Quill. I've already thought up a name for our committee."

"I don't want to join another committee," Quill said. "I don't like committees."

Miriam folded her arms across her chest defiantly. She was in her late fifties, and attractive in a scholarly, middle-aged way that Quill had always found appealing. "Anyone who doesn't support this committee is a male-dominated fascist. It's the Women Against Crimes Against Women committee."

"There haven't been any crimes committed against anybody." Quill said patiently, although this wasn't strictly true. There was an unaccounted-for body in the forensics lab in Syracuse. "No crimes against women, at least. And if there were, I'd be the first one on the picket line to protest. You know that. I told you that in the Chamber meeting."

As she'd expected, the issue of Lovejoy's Nudie Bar and Grill had been instantly politicized, and the Chamber meeting had dissolved into an imbroglio of venomous proportions.

"We're not leaving until we get this settled," Miriam said ominously.

"Fine. First, let's all sit down." Quill pulled one of the chairs away from the round table nearest the bar and waited until they settled. "Would you like coffee? Tea?" She glanced at her watch. It was after twelve, already. "I can send for a bit of lunch, if you'd like."

"I could not eat a thing," Adela said. "I'm dismayed at you, Quill. Dismayed." She slumped forward and stared at the floor. Adela was a big woman with a voice like one of the smaller species of African elephant. She dressed with all the vigor of her considerable personality. Today's pantsuit was peacock blue. She wore a large amethyst pendant smack in the middle of her purple turtleneck. Despite the color, she seemed somehow faded. Adela had never looked faded before.

Quill placed a hand on her forearm. "I think you should have a cup of tea, Adela."

"Why don't you put some arsenic in it?" Carol Ann snarled.

"That's not very nice," Esther said feebly. Esther had dressed for the August weather in a polished cotton sleeveless dress patterned in orange and pink that Quill hadn't seen before. Esther had first pick of the clothes delivered to West's Best Dress Shoppe, of course, and felt modeling the new shipments was an effective sales strategy. She unclipped both her earrings (bright orange hoops) and then clipped them on again.

"Not very nice?" Carol Anne's voice was usually one of the most annoying things about her. It was high, sticky sweet, and precise, not to mention gloating in a spuriously sympathetic way during tax collection season. Except for now. Right now it was low and vicious. She sounded like the ninth Fury with a bad cold. "Not very nice?! With all this stuff about crimes against women we've forgotten about the dirt! These places are filthy! These places are disgusting! I can't believe you let that idiot husband of yours get away with this, Adela."

"How could the mayor have anything to do with this?" Quill said mildly. "And Carol Ann, you can't really think . . ." She stopped herself in mid-sentence. Adela did rule the roost at home.

"You actually have to ask how that fat little slob has anything to do with this?" Carol Ann's face was the red of a third-degree sunburn. She bent forward and hissed like a snake. "He's on the zoning committee, isn't he! He *passed* that license application."

"But he didn't know this morning until Bernie MacAvoy told him!" Adela wailed. "I'm finished in Hemlock Falls. Finished." She looked up from the floor, and some of her old spirit revived. "Of course, Elmer has the best interests of the town at heart." She sat up. "And *I'm* not the Mayor. He is."

"A strip joint in Hemlock Falls?" Miriam demanded. "Whose best interests does that serve, Adela! Cardiologists? Gynecologists? Who!"

Carol Ann screamed, "Eewwww," then yelled, "See! I told you! Filth!"

Quill put her head in her hands.

Adela blinked back tears. "It's clear now that the mayor was tricked. Tricked! It's all the fault of that Internet." She turned on Miriam, "And the library." She raised a purple-clad arm and pointed at the librarian accusingly. "This is your fault!"

"The Internet?" Quill said, bewildered. "The library?"

Miriam glanced at Quill and snapped. "You know how much trouble I had getting the Town Council to approve the funds for the computers so that anyone could go online that wanted to. When I did the presentation I showed them all the sites they could visit to attract new business here. Elmer's been in touch with Maltby by e-mail."

"He never dreamed this would happen," Adela said. "I am in the mayor's confidence, and I advise him occasionally, as you know, although he did not, I repeat, did *not* consult me about this."

"So you say," Carol Ann hissed. "I'll find out the truth, Adela Henry. I always do."

"What did I have to do with this? Elmer assured me that Mr. Maltby had the highest credentials possible. Are you asking me to doubt the words of my husband?"

"What does that mean, 'high credentials'?" Miriam said crossly. "You can't have high credentials. Credentials don't have a size."

"Harvard," Adela said solemnly.

"Harvard my ass!" Miriam shrieked, "Adela. You always have been an idiot!"

"You know," Adela said thoughtfully. "It's odd, isn't it? A topless bar. I wouldn't have thought it of a Harvard man." Miriam threw her arms in the air.

"Well," Quill said briskly. "I honestly think there's not much to worry about. First of all, Hemlock Falls is growing, and businesses like this one are bound to be attracted here. Besides, the MacAvoy place is so out of the way no one's going to be able to find it. And who do we know that would even go there? Maltby will be out of business in a month."

Miriam patted Quill's arm in a very irritating way. "You'd think, with all your experience with men, that you'd know better, Quill."

"All what experience?" Quill said indignantly.

Miriam smiled.

"I cannot believe I am hearing this," Carol Ann said dangerously. She slithered around in her chair and gave the Tavern Lounge a long, slow poisonous glance, as if reassessing the already punishingly high value she'd placed on the building five years before. Then she turned her reptilian gaze on Quill. "You're in favor of naked female dancers, are you?"

"Well, not as such," Quill said. She wasn't sure what she thought about strippers in the abstract, other than having a lot of sympathy for what must be a difficult way of life. "But this is a democracy. And Mr. Maltby's free to go into any legal business he wants to."

Carol Ann flipped her ponytail in contempt, aimed either at the democratic process, freedom, or Quill herself. Probably all three. The scent of her shampoo wafted through the air. Whatever it was, it smelled like Glade air freshner. Maybe it was Glade air freshener. Carol Anne was just weird.

"So what are we going to do about this, Quill?" Adela demanded.

"Action. That's what's needed," Miriam said promptly. She rummaged in the huge canvas tote she carried everywhere and emerged with a yellow pad and pen. "First, we appeal to the zoning commission's decision. I'll ask Howie to help file. And you're communications chief, Quill. We need to get Doreen on some editorials."

"Doreen stays out of the day-to-day business of the *Gazette*," Quill said. "And I'm sure Stoke will have some comment to make without my butting in. And I don't want to be communications chief."

"And we can picket," Esther said in satisfaction. "I

got some very cute Peter Pan blouses in this week at the store. I think we should all be dressed in the same outfit when we picket. There's this very nice teal that would look wonderful on you, Quill."

"I am not going to picket," Quill said firmly. "I am not going to be communications chief. And I am not going to join this committee."

"You aren't going to help?" Miriam said. "I'm astounded. Just astounded."

"Well I'm astounded that you're astounded, Miriam."

Adela, who was nothing if not resilient, had apparently recovered from her personal social humiliation and was ready for battle. She frowned majestically. "I must say that if you are not with us in this, Quill, you are against us."

"There are times when we must all take a stand," Miriam said darkly.

"There are, indeed," Quill said cordially. "And I'm against war, rape, murder, and harassment. This is harassment. I'm against it."

"Harassment!" Miriam said. "You've got to be kidding me."

Quill stood up, preparing to leave. "The man has a perfect right . . ."

". . . To exploit women right here in Hemlock Falls?" Miriam stood up, too. She was shorter than Quill and she stood so close that her gray-blonde curls tickled Quill's chin. "You establishment sellout, you!"

Quill addressed the ceiling. "I have another meeting, ladies. So if you'll excuse me . . ."

"Oh. You're excused all righty," Carol Ann said. "I think we should excuse you from having any more Chamber meetings here at the Inn, for one thing. Ever. I'm treasurer, and I'll see to it."

"And the Ladies Auxiliary luncheon for forty people that we've booked for next week? You can cancel that right now," Adela said. "The heck with this."

"And I'll make sure that the Upstate New York Circulating Librarians' convention goes anywhere but here ncxt month." Miriam widened her big blue eyes—her best feature when they weren't blazing with opprobrium, as they were now. "Solidarity forever!"

"I may have mentioned I have a meeting," Quill said.

"You don't have a meeting," Miriam snapped. "You're backing off. You wimp. I'd like to see you on the barricades at Berkeley!"

"I most certainly *do* have a meeting. And I am *not* backing off. And I was three years old in 1972, so I couldn't have been at Berkeley even if I'd wanted to, which I would have." Quill stuck her chin out. "This is about human rights, too, Miriam. You may not like Maltby's business. I may not like Maltby's business, but it's a free country."

"Bull! A meeting, hah? With whom?" Miriam was a stickler for pronouns, even when infuriated.

"Dina," Quill said, biting back the inclination to add, "so there."

"I'll just bet."

Quill turned and walked out of the Tavern Lounge. By the time she reached the short hall that led to the reception area, she'd taken three deep breaths, counted backwards from ten, and regained some self-possession. By the time she reached Dina and the reception desk, she realized she'd been followed by the entire Committee for Women Against Crimes Against Women. She turned and faced them. "Now what!"

Miriam shoved Quill aside and leaned over the reception desk. "Hello, Dina," she said sweetly. "I hope Quill isn't too late for her meeting."

Dina closed the notebook she'd been scribbling in. She looked at Miriam, beyond Miriam to Adela, Esther, and Carol Ann Spinoza, and finally at Quill. She tapped her teeth with a pencil. "Not so very late," she said cautiously. "But late enough."

"So if you'll excuse us," Quill said, trying to keep the triumph in her voice at a minimum. She nodded toward the oak front door, which was always open in the summer. Miriam hoisted her tote bag to her shoulder and marched off. Adela trudged behind her. Esther looked from Quill to Carole Ann and back again. Then she said, "Oh, dear. Oh, dear," and took off like the White Rabbit. Carol Ann pulled a squeeze bottle of hand antiseptic from her neat white patent-leather purse, rinsed her hands, replaced the bottle with a snap, and exited without a word.

"Wow," Dina said.

"Remind me to give you a raise." Quill put her hands on her head and pushed down, hard. It helped, a little.

"I asked for a raise last month," Dina said. "And you said I was already well over the median pay scale for part-time hotel receptionists. But you were in the middle of that night school course you were taking on small business economics. I guess I should have waited until you forgot all about it. Have you forgotten all about it?"

Quill went past the desk and into her office. Dina rose and followed her and sat on the couch. Quill slumped behind her desk. The desk clock said it was twelve-thirty, which couldn't be right because she felt as if a week had passed since the fire horn had wakened her at four that morning.

"You looked pooped out," Dina said sympathetically. "Why don't you take a nap?"

"You were so great to back up my fib about our meeting, Dina. How did you guess? It was the body language, right?"

"What fib? You mean you fibbed about the committee? You didn't say a word about the committee that I recall. But I know all about it. It was all the shouting in the Tavern Lounge. I didn't actually hear any words. But I called Nate at the bar to see if I should, like, call the cops or whatever, and he said all five of you were going at it like she-bears."

Quill raised tier eyebrows. "She-bears?"

"Don't worry. It's cool. I told Nate he was being a sexist pig."

"And how did Nate respond to . . . never mind. I don't want to know."

"How about your phone calls? Would you like to know about them?" Dina drew a sheaf of pink while-you-were-outs from her jeans pocket.

Quill eyed them warily. "Is there anyone I want to talk to?"

"Well, who don't you want to talk to?"

"Myles."

"Oh, yeah. Because the body wasn't Mr. Maltby's, like you detected."

Quill winced. "Do we know whose body it is?"

"Davy says it turned out to be some small-time hood named Caprese."

"Hm," Quill said intelligently. "That's significant."

Dina's large brown eyes regarded her through her spectacles. "Is it?"

"Well, yes. Of course. A small-time hood named what, again?"

"Named Caprese? Do we know anyone named Caprese?"

Quill admitted that as far as she knew, they didn't. "Did he have a first name?"

Dina looked reproving. "Who said it was a he?"

"It isn't a he? It's a she?"

"Antonia Caprese."

"A female small-time hood?" Quill said, astonished.

"And why not?" Dina said belligerently.

"I didn't think that they . . . you know . . ."

"The Mob."

"The Mob, yes. I thought they were basically male chauvinist pigs."

"That is so dated, Quill. I think you should stop talking gender politics with Miriam and start talking them with me."

"I don't think Miriam's going to be discussing anything with me for a while," Quill said ruefully. "And I'd be delighted to talk gender politics with you anytime."

"Whatever." Dina paged through more pink slips. "Do you want to—"

"I want to know more about Antonia Caprese. Don't you?"

Dina set the pink slips down with a pleased air. "So you finally asked me!"

"Asked you what?"

"To help you and Meg solve a case!"

"I didn't really mean—"

"You know what I think we should do?" Dina took off her spectacles, which were large. and red-rimmed, and sucked thoughtfully on the end of one bow. "I think wc should Google her."

"You mean use the Internet?" Quill nodded. "That's a really good idea."

"It is, isn't it? So, I'll Google her. And then I'll get all the info I can on the police case from Davy. We're supposed to go to the movies tonight, but I'll make him dinner at his place, instead." She smiled happily. "I'll seduce him!"

Quill thought that this would be relatively safe, since Myles didn't share a great deal with his deputy. Solving the darker crimes, like murder, were well down on Davy's personal preference list. "Let's not mention it to Myles, though," she suggested.

"No problem." Dina paged through the slips. "Do you want to talk to the mayor?"

"No."

"Too bad. He seemed pretty pitiful."

"He is pretty pitiful," Quill said indignantly. "I don't know how he could have agreed to give Maltby a license to open a topless bar in Hemlock Falls without discussing the problem with somebody."

Dina lowered the pink slips. "Nate said you thought the nudie bar was just fine."

"I don't think it's fine at all!" Quill felt all her exasperation flooding back. "I think it's a terrible idea. I personally loathe that kind of thing—and talk about exploiting women . . ." Quill shuddered. "Ugh."

"Well, for Pete's sake," Dina said. "Why didn't you say so?"

"I have said so! I'm with Howie Murchison on this one, Dina. But whatever my personal feelings are, the man has a right to do what he wants to do within the law."

"It's like the ACLU defending Nazis," Dina said.

"It's nothing like that at all." Quill picked up her pencil cup and smacked it hard on her desk. "And the ACLU doesn't defend Nazis, Dina, you should know better. They defend the right to free speech. That's different." Quill pulled at her hair. "I don't want to talk about this anymore. Who else called?"

"Denise at Golden Pillar? You want to call her back?"

This was their chief travel agent. "Not if she's got cancellations." Dina set the slip aside. "She's got cancellations?" Quill said, dismayed.

"Two. In December. The Silver Leafers and the

Monteverdi Christmas Reunion."

Those were two huge parties. "Darn."

Dina shook her head sympathetically, "Wow, what with the Chamber canceling all its meetings here, and the librarians not coming . . ."

"Stop," Quill said. "Who else called?"

"Meg." Dina smiled. "This'll cheer you right up. She's down at the Croh Bar and she says Doreen got the three suites filled and the parties are checking in this afternoon."

Quill brightened a little more. "Well, that's good news."

"And she said she wants you to come down to the Croh Bar as soon as you're through with the Chamber meeting. She wants some help moving her stuff out of Andy's. Quill, she's not breaking up with him, is she?"

"Not if I can help it." Quill looked at the desk clock. It was now well after two. "The Chamber meeting was over at twelve. How come you didn't tell me Meg needed me?"

"You were in a meeting with WACAW."

"WA—oh. Women Against . . . fine. Okay. Except I didn't want to be in that meeting at all. Why didn't you tell me Meg was waiting for me?"

Dina blinked at her. "I thought you knew. You came up to the desk with Miriam charging after you like a water buffalo after green algae . . ."

"Dina . . ."

"They like green algae," Dina said. And of course if anyone knew about water buffalo's culinary preferences, it was Dina. "And you asked if you were late for your meeting and I said not much. And by then, you weren't." she craned her head to look at the desk clock. "You are now."

CHAPTER 5

When Marge Schmidt bought the Croh Bar from Darryl Croh and his father Brucie, it was a backwater dive, a dump, a joint that had decades-old, scab-red indoor-outdoor carpeting and smelled like horse pee. It was comfortable, familiar, and Hemlockians loved it. There weren't any flies on Betty Hall, who managed it, or Marge herself, Betty's senior partner. So they scrubbed it down, tore out the old carpeting and put in new, maroon carpeting printed with black medallions and left the rest of it the way it was, except that the food was outstanding and the wine list not bad at all.

Quill found Meg in the booth by the kitchen door in the back. She was drinking Rolling Rock with Jerry Grimsby. Her face was flushed and her dark hair stood on end the way it did when she was cooking well. It was too dark to see the color of her socks, but Quill knew her sister. She was in a scary mood.

"Quill!" Meg leaned across the table and whispered, "It's my sister, Jer."

"Hey, Quill."

"Hey, Meg. I thought you had errands in Ithaca."

Meg lifted a plastic shopping bag. "Mission accomplished. Both missions accomplished, actually, since I got what I needed in Ithaca and I didn't have to go to Syracuse and we've got some new guests checking in this afternoon. And then I ran into Jerry in here."

Quill slid in beside Meg and raised her eyebrows interrogatively at Jerry.

He raised his glass in response. "She's fine. A couple of beers, that's all. She's high as a kite, but it's pre-wedding nerves."

"The heck you say!" Meg said indignantly. "I'm as cool as an English cucumber. As mellow as marrow. As smooth as a swede." She wrinkled her forehead, clearly unable to think of more vegetables. Then she drank more beer.

Jerry laughed. It was a sexy, confident, intimate laugh. Quill frowned at him and he frowned playfully back. "Quill? Bad day at Black Rock? Can I get you a beer? Glass of wine?"

"Not right now, thanks." She folded her hands on top of the table, hoping she looked more casual than she felt. She liked Jerry Grimsby. Almost everybody did. He was tall, burly, with an open face and a ready smile. Like most professional chefs, he'd had a peripatetic career—a chef at a boutique restaurant in New York that had made his reputation, a successful restaurant in San Diego, a brief stint as a recipe critic for *L'Aperitif*, an even briefer season as a celebrity chef on the food channel. A group of investors in Ithaca had brought him in to create a new restaurant in that already over-restauranted city. Jerry called it "Seasons In the Sun" and specialized in fusion foods: Tuscan, Basque, and

Ethiopian. It was a hit, at least for now, and Jerry was on another roll. Seasons was so successful that Quill had wondered a little at his readiness to take over Meg's kitchen while she went off on her honeymoon. Looking at Jerry looking at Meg, Quill wasn't wondering anymore.

Jerry dragged his eyes from her sister's face. "Seems you had a pretty lively time of it up at the Inn this morning."

Quill made a face. "The corpse or the crusade?"

"I heard about the corpse. Somebody named Leo Maltby?"

Quill flushed. "No. No, it's somebody named . . ." she stopped. Was she supposed to know that the corpse was Antonia Caprese, small-time hood? She wasn't sure. She was pretty sure Myles wouldn't think so. "Something else," she finished a little lamely.

"What about this crusade?"

Quill explained, to Jerry's roar of laughter and Meg's confusion.

"A topless bar?" Meg sputtered. "Are you kidding? And what do you mean, 'crusade.' Who's on a crusade?"

Quill recounted Miriam's unsuccessful efforts at recruiting her into the ranks of Women Against Crimes Against Women.

"But we're against crimes against women!" Meg said. "What's the matter with you? And we lost all that business! John's going to be fit to be tied."

At least she didn't look dangerous anymore. She

looked as if flirting with Jerry Grimsby or anyone else was the furthest thing from her mind. She looked cranky. Quill could deal with cranky. "They'll forget all about it in a week," she said optimistically. "Where is Adela going to find cooking as good as yours for the Ladies Fireman's Auxiliary Lunch?"

"Marge's 'Feed America! Diner,' that's where," Meg said flatly. "Those guys could give a rat's behind for my gourmet food. And the Chamber of Commerce? That's a once-a-month deal with a full lunch. Year-round. How are we going to replace that business?"

"Well, there's no other place in Hemlock Falls large enough for a full meeting that will let them have lunch," Quill said. "They'll wind up at the funeral home, like they did before, and after one meeting they'll be back at the Inn. Adela doesn't like to be in a room with the caskets and everyone gets sick of calling out for pizza."

"And the librarians cancelled, too," Meg said crossly. "Honestly, Quill. It's a good thing we've got some new guests coming in this afternoon. Unless you're going to find some way to get rid of them, too."

"Stop," Quill said. "Miriam's going to forget all about this in a few days and everything's going to be fine. Who are the guests, by the way? You didn't by any chance, get the governor's office? He's showing up for the resort opening next week, and if he came to stay with us, it'd be the nuts."

Meg looked shifty. "It's not the governor, no. And actually, it wasn't me. It was Doreen."

"Oh! That's terrific. Her first time out as a booking

agent and she scores three rooms right away. Isn't that great?!"

"Yep."

"So who are they?" Quill waited expectantly.

"It's just some business people. I think they're going to be hiring in the area and they want to scout out the territory. You should ask Doreen about it. I told her she should be the one to let you know."

"Hiring. Even better. Is it their first time with us?"

"Umm. Look, I've got my car loaded with stuff. Are you going to give me a hand?"

"I wonder if we should give Doreen a commission? And of course I'll help you. That's why I'm here."

"I'll help, too," Jerry said cheerfully. "There's just enough time to haul your things home, Meg. I want to be in the kitchen at four."

"I have to be at the Resort Gala Committee meeting at four," Quill exclaimed. "So, yes, Meg. Let's get going. But really, Jerry, please don't trouble yourself. Stay here and finish your beer."

"No trouble at all. It will go a lot faster if I give you a hand. And then you're coming down to the kitchen to show me the ropes, right, Meg?"

"It's just a few suitcases," Quill said. "She's only back for a few days, just until the wedding. You know, Jer—Meg, Andy, marriage. It's why you're here. To help out. While they're on their honeymoon."

Jerry's gaze was sunny, candid, and frank. Quill didn't trust him an inch. "Right. Let's get going, ladies."

He kept a proprietal hand on Meg's arm as Quill followed them out to the parking lot. Once there, she stopped in confusion when she didn't see Meg's car. "Come to think of it, Meg, I didn't see your Escort when I drove in. Where are you parked?"

"The Escort's at the Inn," Meg said with a suspicious defensiveness. "I borrowed Mike's pick-up instead."

"The truck? For three-days' worth of . . ." Quill spotted the familiar blue truck. It was piled high with boxes. Boxes of cookbooks, pottery, shoes, and pillows. "Stuff," Quill said aloud. "It's all your stuff." She stood still for a moment. It was hot and sticky, that was why she felt flushed.

Quill took a time-out, her usual response to shock. The Croh Bar was located smack in the middle of Main Street. From where she stood, she could see both ends of the street. Baskets of blue lobelia hung from the wrought-iron streetlights. Red and pink geraniums bloomed in white planters set along the sidewalks. Most of the buildings on Main were cobblestone, and the late afternoon sun warmed the facades to peach and bronze. She looked at Jerry Grimsby, that big black blot in her particular Eden, and she wanted to growl. She looked at her sister, who was humming an off key version of "For I Am a Pirate King" while she searched her purse for her keys, and she couldn't decide if she wanted to hug her or smack her.

She just made it into the passenger side of the pick-up before Meg gunned the motor and took off. She stopped humming, looked sideways at Quill and demanded,

"What are you doing riding with me? What about your car?"

Quill held on the straphanger as Meg took the turn out of the parking lot at forty miles an hour. The plastic bag Meg'd gotten from Ithaca tumbled into her lap and she pushed it away. It was soft and squishy, and she didn't have time to wonder what was in it. "I'll walk back and get it later. Are you trying to make it back to the Inn in under thirty seconds?"

Meg slowed down. She was a good driver, far better than Quill, who was notoriously absent-minded behind the wheel. "I've got things to do this afternoon." she said virtuously.

"You know, there *are* some wedding things to do, after all," Quill said firmly.

"Not that. I have to be in the kitchen."

Quill pretended she hadn't heard that. "We should really stop by Adela's and check on the flowers one more time, just to be sure she's sent in the order." Adela had added a florist business to her gift shop the year before. Everyone had hoped it would moderate her self-appointed duties as assistant mayor. It hadn't changed a thing.

Meg turned into the long drive that led up to the Inn. "She's probably ordered ragweed, instead of roses. I wouldn't blame her, after you wimped out on her this morning."

"I was standing on principle, not wimping out. Anyway, she'll get over it," Quill said optimistically. "Everyone knows my views on topless bars."

"Why would they necessarily know your views on topless bars?" Meg pulled the truck to a stop by the front door. Behind them, Jerry Grimsby waved as he turned left to park next to the tool shed. Meg stared at his Buick in the rear view mirror, her expression unreadable.

"And it's not as if I'm actively supporting topless bars. I'm not. I mean, I'm not exactly running a recruitment program for strippers, either. But he does have the right to run a legitimate . . ." Meg's expression changed, and Quill interrupted herself. "What's wrong now?"

"Oh, nothing," Meg said airily. She shoved the gearshift into reverse and did a U-turn. "Why don't you hop out here? I'll get Mike to help me get these boxes up to my room. He can schlep them through the dining room. Okay? Bye!"

Quill hopped out, and, frowning, watched Meg roar down the driveway. She skidded around a car coming up the driveway. Quill's frown changed to blank amazement.

It was long, white, and short. It was also square. Quill's visual memory was excellent. She'd seen something like that before, in a television commercial. A Hummer, that was it. Originally designed for the army, to conquer desert sands or whatever. But this was even longer than the standard version. It'd been stretched.

Meg snaked the pick-up expertly by the Hummer and disappeared behind the Inn. The Hummer rolled to a stop. Quill bent down to look through the rolled-up windows and jumped back as the doors opened, seemingly all at once, and four women bounced out onto the pavement.

Quill's first impression was that they were dressed for a far warmer climate than that of Hemlock Falls in August. Such as a clothing-optional beach in the South of France. She hadn't known it was possible to buy shorts that brief. She hadn't known it was possible to buy bras that large, either.

There was a discontented-looking blonde carrying a small white dog, an innocent-faced brunette, and an Asian. Sort of like Charlie's Angels, only much . . . curvier. There was a second blonde; she was older, although Quill didn't know why she was so sure. All four were very, very fit. And smooth. They stood out against the backdrop of the Falls like plastic orchids in a field of daisies.

Once in a while, Doreen would remark approvingly, "Your mamma didn't raise no fools" and Mrs. Quilliam hadn't. It took mere seconds for Quill to realize that this was the advance guard for Lovejoy's Nudie Bar and Grill, and that Doreen had booked them at the Inn for a week.

"Well, hello," she said warmly. "Welcome to the Inn at Hemlock Falls."

"Hiya!" said the blonde with the blue-sequined halter-top and the silver shorts. "I'm Sheree Maltby. And these are the Boom-Boom girls."

"How very nice to meet you, Sheree," Quill said. "We have rooms for you all, of course. Mr. Maltby's already checked in. Will you be staying with him?"

"With my ex? Not hardly!" She winked. Her fake eyelashes were so long they almost brushed her cheeks. "You gotta be Quill, right? The famous artist, like? Right?"

"Well, um, yes."

"And you're gorgeous, too. Doreen was right." She snapped her gum and gave Quill a hug. She smelled of Opium and expensive hair mousse.

"Thank you," Quill said.

"We met your sister at the local dive. She's a cutie, too, isn't she, girls? And your tour director, Doreen. She was there, too. Reminds me so much of my own ma, God bless her, that I almost cried my eyes out when I met her. Both of 'em. Cuties." She put her hands on her hips and surveyed the gardens with warm approval. "This is just the nuts. Will you three look at that water?" She eyed Quill in a friendly way. "You ever been to Vegas? Well, this is almost better than Caesar's Palace. You know, they got a waterfall, too. Fancier than this one, though."

"Put a sock in it, Sheree," said the other blonde. Her haltertop was peacock blue. The sequins were stitched into a concentric pattern with a huge mirrored sequin right in the middle. She held the little Bichon Frise slung over her forearm. It regarded Quill unblinkingly through its fringe. "You got someone to help us with this crap?" She turned, tugged a piece of Louis Vuitton luggage out of the Hummer and slapped it down. "I need a bath and a drink. Like, right now." She looked down at the little dog. "And Tooey got carsick. I think he needs to see a vet." She gave Quill a shrewish glance. "You got a vet in this hick town?"

"We have several. There's a small animal clinic right near the hospital."

The younger blonde shoved the small creature at Sheree. "Here. Make an appointment and take Tooey in. Right away. She's been chucking up for the past hour."

"I warned you what would happen if you fed Tooey chocolates." Sheree smoothed the little dog's ears. "Poor baby."

"Just get it done, will you?"

"Whatever you say, Brittney-Anne." Sheree gave Tooey a kiss on the nose, then tucked him capably under her arm. "You haven't met the rest of us, Quill. This is Brittney-Anne, of course."

"Maltby," Brittney-Anne said crossly. "You, like, always forget the Maltby."

"Right," Sheree said, her wide smile dimming a fraction. "Leo's wife. And that's Candi and Taffi. With an 'I'."

Sheree had to be close to forty. The others appeared to be somewhere in their twenties. They were all extremely glamorous rather than beautiful, except for Brittney-Anne. She was flat-out gorgeous, in the way that people like Elizabeth Taylor were gorgeous. Her eyes were an astonishing turquoise blue.

"How nice to meet you all," Quill said. "If there's anything we can do for you while you're here, please let us know."

"A coupla things, since you asked," Sheree said. "You gotta local paper, don't you?"

"The *Gazette*, yes."

"Doreen said she could get me a break on some advertising space."

"I'm sure she can."

"I'm in charge of recruitment and we're going to run a coupla ads. Not just in the locals, of course. We'll cover five or six counties."

"Ads?" Quill repeated. "Five or six counties?"

"Yeah. Leo figured it'd drum up a bit of excitement if we used a coupla local girls in the act, so I want to make as big a splash as I can in Hemlock Falls. I was thinking maybe a full-page spread, you know? We always get a big response when I go all out with the spread." Sheree waved one well-manicured hand in the air. " 'Big Boobs? Make Big Bucks!' "

"I beg your pardon?" Quill said, startled.

"The headline," Sheree said kindly. "Anyhow, like I said, we always get a hundred, maybe two hundred kids think they can make it in exotic dancing and I'm gonna need space to see how they handle the routines."

"How many?" Quill took a deep breath. There didn't seem to be enough air outside. "Hundreds?"

"Oh, yeah. We'll get them from as far away as Syracuse. I let 'em all try out." Sheree's tone became kindlier still. "Most of 'em couldn't cut mustard with a knife, but it's good PR, you know? Get's everybody interested."

"Leo's a genius at PR," Brittney-Anne added. "Knows how to get the TV stations out here and everything. Says good PR is what it's all about."

Quill nodded. She bit her lip. When that didn't work, she pinched her ear, hard.

Sheree smiled at her. It was a friendly smile, and Quill couldn't help but return it. "So. You got a space we can maybe use?"

"Not for hundreds, no," Quill said apologetically. She had a brief vision of the local high school gym. She had an even briefer vision of an outraged Adela Henry, picketing the Inn. "I'll try and think of something," she promised. "Please come in, won't you? And we'll get you settled."

Except for Brittney-Anne, all of them obediently clopped toward the front door. Taffi and Candi wore stiletto heels that were six inches high. Sheree's shoes were six inches high, too, but the heels were acrylic with little goldfish swimming around in them. Quill hoped the goldfish were fake.

Brittney-Anne stayed put and raised her voice to a petulant yowl. "Somebody's gotta park my flippin' car!" Everybody stopped. Taffi rolled her eyes. Candi made a face. Sheree gave them both a minatory look. "Don't worry about the car, Brit."

"She means Brat," Candi hissed, *sotto voce.*

"She means Bitch," Taffi snickered.

"Cut it out," Sheree said.

"And there'd better not be a scratch on it after they do."

"We'll get Mike to take care of it," Quill promised.

"So who's gonna get me a drink, too?" Brittney-Anne shoved her way past the others and swayed up the steps to the thick oak door. "See to the booze, Sheree, right? Send it up to Leo's suite. And gimme the goddam dog." Tooey squeaked in protest as she grabbed him from Sheree's comforting grasp. "The shit I have to put up with around here, Tooey." The turquoise gaze swiveled to Quill. "Leo's checked in awready, you said. The suite, ri—"

"If you mean Mr. Maltby," Quill said hastily, "yes. He's checked in. Just ask for the key to 331 at the desk."

Max chose that moment to come trotting out the front door, just as Britney-Anne was swaying in on her stiletto heels. He stopped. His ears went up. He plunged forward and poked an amiable nose in Tooey's direction. Tooey struggled in Brittney-Anne's grasp and yapped hysterically. Brittney-Anne extended one well-shaped leg and kicked out. "Get away from here you flippin' mutt!"

Max dodged, cowered, wagged his tail in canine apology, and took off for the ravine.

Candi flipped her glossy black hair and muttered a word Quill never used in reference to other women.

It was going to be a very long week.

CHAPTER 6

Quill knew she should walk right into the foyer and give her receptionist a hand with checking in the Boom-Boom girls.

On the other hand, Dina had once checked forty-three members of the XXXtreme All-Male Wrestling tour into all twenty-seven rooms in twenty-two minutes flat. She'd handle the Boom-Boom girls with aplomb, no doubt about that at all.

But Dina would also handle it with a lot of questions about silicone implants, work habits, and pay rates. She was a curious person. She'd been considering a career change. She was getting tired of copepods and their extremely lengthy lifecycle. The Boom-Boom girls had a lot of celebrity-style glitz when compared to the life-cycles of microscopic creatures that lived in algae-infested freshwater ponds. What if Dina fell for the glamour of the outside world and quit to join the world of sleazy showbiz?

Worse yet, what was going to happen when Doreen ran into the snotty Brittney-Anne? Could the kitchen handle it when the dining room became jammed with Hemlockians desperate (for disparate reasons) for a glimpse of all that bosomy flesh? Poor Jerry Grimsby hadn't signed on for riot and revolution.

A responsible innkeeper would march right in there and mediate, moderate, and deflect. The least she could do was turn up the air conditioning so the Boom-Boom girls would have to put on sweaters.

Quill didn't feel up to it. She was tired. She'd had a long day. She had thirty minutes left to shower, change, and get to the Resort Gala Committee meeting by four o'clock. There just wasn't time. And she was not, Quill told herself, wimping out. Not at all.

She went around the side of the Inn to the fire escape and trudged up three flights of stairs to her rooms. Nobody stopped her. She didn't hear any shrieks of dismay from the kitchen; in the hall, she saw no sign of Meg or Jerry or Meg's worldly belongings. Good. Her sister was sensible underneath all the hysteria. She was probably on her way back to Andy's right now.

Quill slipped into her own rooms like a fox that had escaped the hunt. She checked her watch; twenty-five minutes to get to the Resort Gala Committee. If she were really, really rotten, she could call Elmer on his cell phone, cough weakly into the phone, and plead a sudden catastrophic flu. But she'd have to stay in bed for at least twenty-four hours, and Dina, Meg, Doreen, Bjarne, and anybody else with a problem or a fit of temper would march right into her bedroom and stay there until it was fixed. They'd done it before.

All she really wanted was a nap. The Resort Gala Committee was definitely the lesser evil. With any luck, she could sit in the back and let everyone else talk. She walked into her bedroom and opened her closet.

One of the first habits she'd acquired when she and Meg bought the Inn more than ten years ago was something she thought of as Intentional Minimalism. Every physical requirement in her personal life was set up to deliver the least amount of hassle and minimize decision making. She owned fifteen sets of exactly the same kind of underwear so that she didn't have to think about laundry more than once every two weeks. And she had innkeeper uniforms, divided by season. The summer innkeeper uniform consisted of five tea-length silk skirts in varying shades of bronze, cinnamon, heavy cream, sage, and primrose. She owned ten silk tee-shirts that went with the skirts. It made deciding what to wear very easy. It made Myles laugh.

Quill grabbed a skirt and tee-shirt and was showered, dressed, and back down the fire escape to the parking lot in fifteen minutes. She looked for her car. She remembered, too late, that her car was in the parking lot at the Croh Bar a mile and a half away. If she walked back into the Inn and asked for a ride, she'd get caught up in the catastrophe of the moment. It would be faster to jog.

By the time she got through Peterson Park to her Honda, she was sweaty, her silk tee shirt was wrinkled, and her hair was falling all over her face. She pinned it back up in a haphazard fashion and checked her watch. Four-thirty. Ten minutes to drive to the resort and an hour for the meeting. With any luck at all, she'd be back at five-thirty, in time to take Doreen, Dina, and Meg to Elise's in Ithaca for dinner. Elsie's was the perfect place to have a relaxed, beautifully prepared meal. Quill particularly liked the booths, which were ideal for quiet discussions. There were two topics on Quill's quiet-discussion list: Doreen's new job description and Meg's pre-wedding nerves. She'd handle both of them with tact and diplomacy. And then maybe they would let her take a nap. The booths were great for napping.

She drove down the curving road to the Resort at Hemlock Falls with the happy sense that things were under control. The Boom-Boom girls could take care of themselves. She could take care of Meg and Doreen.

She pulled into a parking space, noting in passing that there were a lot more vehicles here than she'd expected, but mostly astonished at the progress on the resort since March. The last time she'd been down here had been during the ROCOR v. Meecham trial, and the place had been a mess. Now the hotel was up and the sod was laid and four large gazebos lined the beach on the Hemlock River.

Quill got out of the car and looked around. The place was impressive. If upstate New York had an architectural style, it was what Quill mentally stigmatized as "Victorian Lake." There was Ugly Victorian Lake (local limestone dyed dark red and a flurry of gingerbread trim), and Pretty Nice Victorian Lake (local limestone left its natural gray-beige and neatly simple trim). This was pretty nice. The limestone was a mellow cream; the architects had painted the window frames, eaves, and doors off-white; the roofs were a dark green shingle. Quill stood in the parking and looked at it all with mild pleasure.

"There you are, Quill! I told you not to be late, and here you are, late as usual." Elmer hurried down the broad concrete steps and grabbed her by the elbow.

"I'm sorry," Quill allowed herself to be dragged up the steps into the foyer. "It's only five minutes past the half-hour. Well, fifteen. Elmer, this looks very nice. It ought to be a real asset for us. You must be really happy." She shook her elbow free and looked around the hotel interior. There was an atrium in the middle, and it soared up all six stories to a set-in glass roof. August sunshine flooded the granite floors. "This is very nice, too."

"No offense, Quill. But aren't you going to do something about your hair?" Elmer had taken hold of her elbow again and was dragging her toward the back of the foyer. It was in shadow, but Quill could make out a crowd of people milling around a lectern.

"My hair?" Quill patted it, then stuck a few hairpins more firmly in place. "This is just a regular meeting, Elmer." She thought a moment, then added indignantly. "And why are you making rude comments about my hair?"

"We got an opportunity, here," Elmer said importantly. "And it's *not* a regular meeting. Carpe . . . carpe . . . you know."

Quill stared at him blankly. "Fish?" she said. "Why are you talking about fish?"

"Too late now." Elmer raised his voice, "Well, folks! Here she is!" His shove may have been intended to be gentle, but it caught her unaware. She stumbled forward and steadied herself on the lectern. Ferris Rodman grasped her arm and pulled her up to the podium.

Quill, confused, took a moment to orient herself. She looked down at Elmer, who gave her a stupid grin. She turned to Ferris Rodman, whose grin wasn't stupid at all, but slightly sinister. She hadn't seen Ferris Rodman since the ROCOR v. Meecham trial. He was the developer behind the Resort At Hemlock Falls, and responsible for one of the scarier incidents in Quill's career as an amateur detective. He looked like a mild-mannered middle-aged civil engineer, but Quill knew better. He was middle-aged, and a civil engineer, but he was as mild-mannered as a grizzly bear in April.

Quill squinted over the lectern to the people standing in front of it. The lights were bright. A young guy with long black hair and a Steadicam balanced on his shoulder looked bored. He stood next to a thin, fortyish blonde whose face was very familiar. Angela Stoner, from Channel 15 in Syracuse, that's who it was. Angela carried a note pad and she waggled her fingers at Quill. Quill waggled back. There were a couple of college kids with video cameras and tee-shirts labeled CORNELL UNIVERSITY PRESS.

Quill chuckled. It looked like she was in the middle of a press conference.

Ferris Rodman nudged her politely aside and leaned into the microphone. "I'd like to welcome you all to this press conference covering the long-awaited opening of the Resort at Hemlock Falls."

Quill stared at him. It *was* a press conference. What was she doing at a press conference?

Rodman swept the room with a genial glance. "Now,

we here in Hemlock Falls know that there's been some concern expressed in the statewide news about a purposed exotic dancer bar in the area . . ."

"This a pre-emptive strike, Rodman?" Angela Stoner called out.

Rodman's geniality was unimpaired. "You could call it that. We want to reassure the citizens of Tompkins County . . ."

"And your investors?" Angela interrupted with a wolfish grin.

Rodman ignored this and continued smoothly, "We'd like to reassure the folks both here and in the great state of New York that Hemlock Falls remains a wonderful place to visit. We have some of the best vineyards, the greatest food, the finest hostelries anywhere in the United States."

Hostleries? Quill thought. Good grief.

"Cultural arts, too," Rodman said. "Which, unlike this proposed exotic dancer's bar, dominate our recreational life here. And I know you're all anxious to meet Sarah Quilliam, an exemplar of the arts and culture I just reviewed for you. She'll speak to you for about twenty minutes about the role of art here in Hemlock Falls. She'll be followed by a performance of the Ladies Auxiliary Choir and an address by the mayor. There will be time for questions."

Exemplar? Quill blinked at him. Then she got dizzy. Somehow, someway, she'd gotten caught up in a public relations battle between the town and Lovejoy's Nudie Bar and Grill. And she'd bet her last nickel on who had leaked the news to the statewide press: that miserable cur Leo "Boom-Boom" Maltby himself, who, at this very moment, was probably enjoying the favors of that snippy brat Brittney-Anne in the best suite at her Inn. And she'd bet her second-to-last nickel on who had the bright idea to strike back with a bunch of hooey about culture. Carpe diem her aunt Fanny. She glared down at Elmer.

Ferris Rodman smiled easily at the audience. "Some of you may already know that Sarah and her sister Margaret run the nationally known Inn at Hemlock Falls. And I'm sure some of you know of Quilliam, the highly regarded, reclusive artist who retired from the arts scene in New York some years ago after a short, brilliant career. Now all of you know that Hemlock Fall's own Sarah Quilliam, and that Quilliam are one and the same." Ferris turned, leading the markedly unenthusiastic applause. "Quill? Tell us why Hemlock Falls inspires the best of your highly regarded work."

Quill opened her mouth. Then she closed it. She mashed some of her straggling hair over her left ear. She sucked her lower lip between her teeth and coughed.

The silence was excruciating.

She looked at the ceiling and said, "Welcome to Hemlock Falls, ladies and gentlemen," in an icky, Jackie Kennedy whisper. She cleared her throat and tried again. This time her voice came out as a shout. "Mr. Rodman will be glad to answer any questions. Thank you!"

She jumped off the podium and fell against the mayor.

"That was your speech?" Elmer said. "Holy moly, Quill. You looked like a idiot up there. No offense," he added hastily. Then he got a glimpse of her expression, and began to back up.

Quill righted herself. She grabbed Elmer by his Best-Little-Village-in-New-York tie and brought his face so close to hers she could identify the brand of his toothpaste. She was so mad she couldn't talk. Instead she jerked Elmer's head from side to side.

"Gaah," Elmer said. Then, in a strangled squeak, he complained, "The cameras are rolling."

Quill glared over her shoulder. The guy with the Steadicam was rolling tape. Angela Stoner gave her a thumbs up. Quill released Elmer's tie.

Elmer readjusted his tie with a pained expression and whispered, "What are you so all-fired mad about?"

"Are you *kidding me?!*"

"Hush," Elmer said nervously. He plastered a big smile on his face and nodded vigorously in the direction of the Channel 15 Steadicam. "She'll be with you in a minute, folks. Just a little misunderstanding."

"Misunderstanding?" Quill struggled for calm. She really did.

"I left a phone message for you," Elmer said in a rapid, bewildered undertone. "A couple of 'em. And I left you all the particulars. How Ferris there said you were famous all over the U.S. of A. and that we'd get better press coverage if the stations knew you were coming. All we wanted was for you to say a few words, Quill. About why you picked Hemlock Falls when you retired from painting. About why other people should come and see it. Although," he added ruminatively, "how famous can you be if the only press that came out here is the kids from Cornell and Channel 15? Tell you what," he stuck his lower lip out in an aggrieved pout, "I been sold a bill of goods here." He sighed. "Anyway. In my last message I said there wasn't any need to call back if you were going to come. So I thought we were all set."

Quill took a deep breath. "I didn't get the message."

"Sorry," Elmer muttered. "Sorry, sorry, sorry. Boy, it's been one heck of a day." He rubbed the back of his neck. He looked like Max dodging a kick from Brittney-Anne, the Boom-Boom girl.

Quill exhaled. "Okay."

"You mean you'll do it?"

"Sure. Fine. Whatever."

"You'll talk about why you moved to Hemlock Falls?"

"Yes!" Quill said crossly. She was furious with Elmer, but not furious enough to embarrass him in front of Channel 15. He'd had a hard day. And she could talk for a long time about Hemlock Falls. She did it all the time when tour groups checked in. It'd be great publicity for the Inn.

Elmer grinned all over. He reached up and tugged at Ferris Rodman's chinos. "She's ready," he hissed. "Just a few womanly nerves."

Quill opened her mouth to protest and shut it. She'd take care of Elmer later.

Rodman wrapped up his speech in a few sentences, reintroduced Quill in even fewer, and she got up behind the lectern again. She rubbed her nose furiously. "Well," she said. "You've been welcomed to Hemlock Falls twice already, so I won't do that again."

She paused, hoping for an appreciative chuckle. Somebody sighed. Somebody else coughed. The guy with the Steadicam yawned.

Quill smiled into the lights. "You can see for yourselves how lovely it is here. Now, in high summer, it is especially beautiful. But there is beauty every . . ."

A hand shot up. Angela Stoner.

"Um. Yes, Angela?"

"What can you tell us about the body off Stalker road?"

"Off Stalk . . . oh, you mean the MacAvoy place."

"Whatever."

That was an easy one. "All inquiries regarding that should be referred to the sheriff's department."

"Aren't you personally involved with this sheriff? What's his name . . ." The woman from Channel 15 paged through her notebook. "Myles McHale."

"No comment," Quill said, in her best defense-attorney style. She knew that all those episodes of *Law and Order* hadn't been a waste of time. "But I can tell you that the body has been removed to the forensics lab in Syracuse. Identification should be made public fairly soon."

"So you *do* know the identity of the victim."

Quill grasped the edges of the lectern, just like Sam Waterston facing a crowd of hostile reporters. "I'm afraid we can't comment on that at this point in time."

Ferris Rodman gently nudged her to one side. "I think we want to keep our focus on the issue at hand, Ms. Stoner. Which is the opening of my new resort. Is there another question?"

One of the young women from Cornell raised her hand shyly. "I'm an art student, Miss Quilliam. And I just wanted to ask, do you ever, like, offer critiques? I've been working a lot in acrylics myself, and of course, my professor says you're one of our best artists in that medium. Although, frankly, I can't see it. Anyhow, *I'm* available if you want to talk about it."

"Does anyone," Ferris Rodman said desperately, "have a question about the resort?"

A fat, hairy hand shot up from the rear of the crowd. It held a cigar between two fingers.

"Mr. Maltby," Quill said, surprised. Then she scowled ferociously. "I've got something to say to you."

"Not him!" Elmer hissed. "Jeez, Quill!"

Leo's grin was as broad as Hemlock Gorge. "Right you are. Leo 'Boom-Boom' Maltby. That's M-A-L-T-B-Y, folks. You got a minit? I got a couple of things to say." Leo came forward, handing out what looked like press kits right and left. His method of working through crowds was definitely tactile. He slapped a few backs, pinched Angela Stoner on the cheek, and leered at the art student who didn't think much of Quill's work in acrylics. He stopped directly under the microphone and looked up at Quill. "Seems like I got you to thank for the only support I got in this town, dolly."

"You do?" Quill said.

Leo swung himself onto the podium with surprising agility. He placed his forefinger in the center of Ferris Rodman's chest. Rodman backed up, startled. Leo brought his face close to the microphone. "I got a coupla announcements to make myself, folks. Just open the press kits I've given out and take a look at this!"

"Scum!" somebody shrieked.

Leo pulled a glossy, four-color eight-by-ten photo from the press kit. It was a studio shot of Brittney-Anne in full exotic-dancer dress. A fan of purple feathers did not conceal the fact that her bosom owed a lot to Du Pont, and very little to nature. A second purple fan failed to make up for Brittney-Anne's flat derriere. Quill suppressed a "ha!" of mean-spirited satisfaction. The color was extremely flattering, though.

"Exploiter!" somebody else shouted.

Quill pulled her attention from the press kit and directed it to the back of the room. Those shrieks were familiar. "Rat-fink!" a third voice chimed in.

"What the heck?" Elmer said.

Ferris Rodman shoved Elmer unceremoniously aside and stared at the mass of women headed toward Leo Maltby and his press kit. Most of them held signs. Those who didn't hold signs held tomatoes. "Who *are* those people?"

"The one with the 'Women Against Crimes Against

Women' sign is Miriam Doncaster," Quill said. "The one with the sign reading 'Perverts Go Home' is Carol Ann Spinoza. The one with . . ." she winced. Adela Henry and Carol Ann Spinoza had reached the dais. They grabbed Leo by the knees. Adela shouted, "A-one, a-two, a-three!" and she and Carol Ann pulled Leo off the platform and onto the ground. Then they whacked him with Adela's sign.

A tomato sailed through the air and landed splat in the middle of Elmer's Best-Little-Village tie. Carol Ann punched Leo in the nose. And Ferris Rodman strode back into the room with two of his truckers at his side.

Quill let out her breath. It was definitely time to go home.

"It's not funny," Quill said an hour-and-a-half later. Dina, Meg, and Doreen sat on the couch in her suite like a troop of baboons in a *National Geographic* wildlife special: giggling, pointing, and pounding each other on the back was very typical of the species. Quill herself remained aloof and dignified in her Eames chair.

All four of them were watching the seven o'clock news on Channel 15. Angela Stoner's headline had been delivered with a smirk: "Fruit Flies At Nudie Protest." At least Angela hadn't identified the tomatoes as vegetables. That always bugged Quill.

"I told you to get a haircut!" Meg shrieked as the TV camera lingered on Quill's open-mouthed astonishment. "You look like you were caught in a riot."

"I *was* caught in a riot," Quill said crossly.

Meg still had the plastic bag she'd been carrying around all day. She pounded it with both fists as Adela mashed tomatoes all over Leo Maltby's face. "Go get 'em, Adela!"

Earlier in the fray, well-known artist Sarah Quilliam had her own comments to make on the plans to open an exotic dancer business in her little town, Angela Stoner told the camera. The tape switched to Quill's attempt to throttle Elmer.

"I think your hair looks great," Dina said loyally. "Messy is very in. And I always, like, hated that tie the mayor's wearing. I'd have tried to rip it off him, too, Quill. But maybe not on national TV."

"Channel 15 is not national TV," Quill said stiffly. "It's local. Very, very local. Hardly anybody watches it."

"Everybody I know watches it," Doreen said.

I'm afraid we never did get to the opening of the Resort At Hemlock Falls, folks, Angela Stoner said into the camera. *The hottest news of the day features an even hotter spot in this small town Eden.*

Quill punched the off button on the clicker and Angela's face winked out. Meg grabbed the clicker and turned the TV back on.

"Wow," Dina said after a few moments. "That Carol Ann's got a good right hook on her. No wonder Mr. Maltby needed all that gauze. Noses bleed like anything."

The story concluded with Angela Stoner's smirky

smile, a still shot of Brittney-Anne's considerable cleavage from the press kit Leo Maltby had given out at the press conference, and Angela's cheerily insinuating voice-over: *We'll keep you abreast of current developments.*

"Oh, ha ha," Quill said sourly. She punched the off button and this time nobody said a thing.

"I didn't know that Women Against Crimes Against Women had so many members," Dina said. "And they just ran right in and started whacking everybody over the head with those signs?"

"Yep." Quill tossed the clicker onto the oak chest she used as a coffee table and stood up. "Leo Maltby was blatting away to the cameras making Sodom and Gomorrah sound like a Disneyland attraction next to the plans for Lovejoy's Nudie Bar and Grill. Next thing I knew, we were invaded. Miriam sailed in followed by at least fifteen really ticked off women. Most of them carried signs like the one Adela used to belt Leo. 'No to Smut!' and 'Drive Out the Dive!' Well, you saw it for yourselves. They were made of yardsticks with cardboard stapled to them. The signs weren't really dangerous. And Carol Ann was the only one who actually socked anyone. I don't know why Leo got a nosebleed. He must be extra sensitive. Anyhow, Ferris Rodman and a couple of his guys broke it up. I'm just glad nobody called the cops."

Meg shook her head. "And the cameras were rolling all that time?"

Quill gestured toward the now-silent television. "You

saw it for yourselves. Although it wasn't as bad as all that. The station edited the footage down, obviously. The only person hurt was Leo Maltby."

"The man of the hour. The most popular guy in the village right now. And he thanked you for your support right on camera." Dina shook her head. "I'm just glad the WACAWs weren't there to hear him say that, Quill. You might have gotten smacked on the nose, too."

"Oh, everyone'll catch it on the news, just as we did," Meg said cheerfully. "So. What now? We throw Maltby out, right? I mean, who needs all this aggravation?"

"I was already going to throw Maltby out as soon as I had half a minute to myself. I told you how he harassed Dina," Quill said. "But now I'm thinking we should keep him here, if we can."

Meg rolled her eyes. "Yuck."

"Does he even want to stick around?" Dina said. "I mean, if Adela Henry were after me with a yardstick, I'd leave in two seconds flat."

Doreen snorted. "I could take that Adela with one hand tied behind my back. But I gotta agree. The guy ain't got much moxie to him. I see him checking out this minute if not sooner. Did you see how he ran off when Carol Ann come after him a second time?"

Quill shook her head. "I run off when Carol Ann comes after me with an attitude, much less her purse. That purse is a lethal weapon. Do you know how heavy it is? It's all that disinfectant she carries. No, I think Maltby's got plenty of courage. Too much, maybe. You'd think he'd want to keep a lower profile."

"Guys like that are always sneaky cowards," Meg said skeptically. "He's got half the town after his blood. He'll be out of here in a New York minute."

"We could lock him up in Meg's and my office," Doreen said. "Easy enough."

Quill suppressed a shudder. "You're missing the point, guys. I don't want Leo Maltby to go anywhere. I want him right here, where we can keep an eye on him."

"Uh-oh," Meg said with a grin. "Here it comes."

"It's logical, isn't it?" Quill began to pace up and down the length of her small living room. "Who else could have killed Antonia Caprese?"

"I thought you'd get around to the murder sooner or later," Meg said.

Quill raised her forefinger. "First thing. The gold cigar lighter was found at the scene of the crime." She raised another finger. "Second thing. He carries the darn lighter like it's some sort of talisman. He's never without it. Third thing . . ." She trailed off. Everyone looked at her expectantly. "Well, it was found at the scene of the crime."

"You just said that," Meg pointed out.

"And if we prove he killed Antonia Caprese, he'll go to jail and a convicted felon can't run a business in New York State."

"They can't?" Dina asked. "What about Jeffery Skilling? Dennis Koslowski? Kenneth Lay?"

"Well, none of *them* should be able to run a business in New York State, either. If Maltby's convicted of murder, how's he going to have time to run a topless bar?"

"I thought you were for the topless bar," Dina said. "You said so on national TV. Now you don't want the topless bar?"

"I am for freedom of speech, and freedom of business and any other freedom that doesn't hurt anyone else," Quill said. "I thought I made that perfectly clear. And I am against discrimination of any kind. I am also against civil unrest. And Maltby's absolutely encouraging people to riot. Who do you think leaked the news about the Grill to the press? Who do you think tipped off Miriam and Adela and Carol Ann about the press conference? Maltby, that's who. He *wants* all this upset!"

"Why?" Meg asked.

"I have no idea. But I'd be an idiot to stand up for a guy who positively asks people to throw tomatoes at him. So I'm standing up for the idea of the Grill. But I'm not standing up for Maltby."

Meg yawned. Dina cast a surreptitious glance at a copy of *Elle* Quill had on the coffee table. Doreen seemed to be napping.

Quill decided she wasn't going to defend her principles anymore. Nobody ever listened to her, anyway. "And you're all forgetting the most important thing: he may be a murderer, in addition being friends with a boob-pincher."

"It wasn't Mr. Ferguson who pinched me, it was Mr. Maltby," Dina said. "But I think this investigation is a very good idea. I agree with you about murderers." She folded her hands on her lap and looked at Quill expectantly. "So how do we start?"

Meg set her plastic bag on the floor and eased herself up off the couch. She'd changed out of her shorts and tee-shirt and was wearing black silk pants and an extremely sophisticated black blouse with a rhinestone rose on the pocket. She looked terrific. "What if he didn't do it? Myles interviewed him after Antonia Caprese's body was discovered in the fire, didn't he? And he didn't arrest him. Maybe he has an alibi."

Quill stopped in mid-stride. After a moment, she said, "I didn't think about that. But this isn't a case you solve just like that." She snapped her fingers. "I'm sure there's more evidence to be gathered."

"Of course Leo did it," Dina said indignantly. "The guy's a sleazola."

"Not all sleazolas are murderers," Quill said. Then, with a vague recollection of her course in Logic 101 she added, "Although all murderers are sleazolas. Okay, so we have to find out who killed Antonia Caprese and hope like heck it was Leo Maltby."

"I'm cool with it," Dina said.

"I'm cool, too," Doreen said. She too, had changed out of her workday gear, and was dressed in a very nice black pantsuit. Quill had been so wrapped up in the events of the past several hours that she'd failed to register this unusual behavior until now.

"Dinner," she said in dismay. "I forgot I was going to take you all to dinner at Elise's."

"Change in plans," Meg said briskly. "I'm taking you

to dinner. And not to Elise's. We're already late. I made reservations at seven-thirty and it'll take half an hour to get there."

Quill looked at her watch.

"I do think," Dina said, "that, like, a murder investigation is more important than food."

"That's 'cause you're twenty-two years old." Doreen put her hands on her knees and hoisted herself off the couch with a groan. "I'm so hungry, my stomach thinks my throat is cut."

"Where are we going?" Suddenly, Quill remembered Meg's quietly mysterious behavior that morning. The trip to Ithaca. Her suspiciously eager agreement to eat at somebody else's restaurant. She looked sharply at her sister. Meg gazed limpidly back. "I'll just brush my hair and then we'll go."

"This is how you guys investigate murders?" Dina said. "By stopping for dinner?"

"There is nothing," Meg said, "more important than this dinner." She picked up the plastic bag off the floor and waved it at them. "And forget about brushing your hair, Quill. Your hair's taken care of."

CHAPTER 7

"I've heard about this place," Dina said. "But it's so expensive, I've never been here before."

All four of them were in a back booth at Jerry Grimsby's restaurant, Seasons in the Sun. Dina and Doreen sat across from Meg and Quill. Meg was wearing a blonde wig. The hair fell to her shoulders. Quill was wearing a wig, too. Her wig was gray and short.

"Tell me again about the wigs?" Quill said. The one she had on was very itchy.

"Ssh!" Meg said rudely. "Where is that waiter, anyhow?" She was also wearing a pair of drugstore spectacles, the kind that offer nonprescription magnification for people with presbyopia. Meg didn't have presbyopia, as far as Quill knew, and she had to hold the menu up to her nose to read it through the lenses. They were a very distinctive pair. The frames were red plastic hearts.

"She's in disguise, Quill." Dina shoved her own glasses up her nose with her forefinger. "So she can write a review of the restaurant."

"I know that," Quill said crossly. "Why do *I* have to wear a wig? Nobody here knows me. The only person here who knows me is Jerry and he's not here because he's cooking in your kitchen, Meg." It was stupid to ask if Jerry knew Meg was at his restaurant in a blonde wig. Of course he didn't.

"After tonight's news, you're notorious," Meg said. "Everyone knows you by sight, by now."

"And why did I get the gray wig?"

"Because you're older than I am. And shh! Here comes the waiter, finally." She looked at her watch, then made a note in a little pad she'd laid by her dinner plate. "Twenty minutes we've been sitting here," she said merrily. "Bad, bad, bad."

The waiter was tall, young, and had a ring in his left nostril. "Welcome to Seasons, ladies. Sorry for the delay. The kitchen's a little backed up. My name is Tom, and I'm here to serve you."

Meg scribbled furiously in her notebook. Quill sighed. She didn't have to read the notes to know what they said. No dining guest should know a thing about the state of the kitchen. And wait service should be discreet, unobtrusive, and utterly silent. The waitstaff at Hemlock Falls were forbidden to introduce themselves to patrons.

Meg stabbed a final period in her book, looked up and said cheerily, "Hi, Tom. My friend and I are taking our mothers out for a nice meal."

"Your what?" Quill said. Dina didn't look like anyone's mother. Even a gray wig wouldn't make her look old enough to be anyone's mother. "Do you mean me?"

"Shut up, Mom." Meg wiggled her eyebrows at Dina. "It's a special day, isn't it Dina?"

Dina smiled cheerfully. "And we wanted to share it with our moms. You betcha."

Meg leaned toward Tom in a confiding way. "We've heard this place is pretty good, Tom."

"Thank you, miss."

"Almost as good as that place up the road a bit. The Inn at Hemlock Falls?"

"Probably better than that, miss. Have you tried their duck?" He shook his head sorrowfully.

Quill froze.

Dina squeaked.

Doreen said, “T’uh!”

Meg smiled like a short blonde shark. “My mom will have a double martini, straight up, two olives, Tom.”

“I what!” Quill said.

“And what would your mom like, Dina?”

Dina giggled. “I don’t know. What d’ya think, Mom?” She nudged Doreen with her elbow.

“I’ll have one a them, daughter,” Doreen said, nudging her back. “The same thing Myra’s got.”

“Myra?” Quill said. “Myra?”

“You do like your gin, Myra,” Doreen cackled.

“And I’ll have a bottle of the Buttonwood Meritage, ’97, Tom. Will you split it with me, Dina? Good. Thank you, Tom.” Meg nodded dismissively. “We’ll think about our starters while you get our drinks, Tom.”

Tom nodded, wheeled around, and walked off. Quill took the table knife, inserted the blade under her hairline and scratched her head as unobtrusively as possible.

“Stop that, missy!” Doreen grumbled. “That’s revolting.”

“So’s a double martini,” Quill said. “So’s this wig. Meg, I still don’t understand what you think you’re up to.”

“She’s starting a career as a restaurant critic,” Dina said kindly, “because Jerry Grimsby’s running the kitchen and she’s going to be at home waiting for Andy all the time, and she doesn’t want to be unemployed.”

“You explained that in the car,” Quill said. “Meg . . .”

She stopped, not sure how to continue. Meg knew perfectly well the kitchen was her kitchen and nobody else's. Did she want to stop cooking and become a restaurant critic? Was that what this was all about? "You'll make a brilliant restaurant critic." She stopped again. The stupid wig must be making it hard to think. That and fatigue. She'd gotten up at four in the morning, for goodness' sake. And been in a minor riot at the new resort. No wonder nothing made sense.

Quill shoved the wig further up her head. Meg had always been a creature of her emotions. No, her sister was more complicated than that: Meg knew she existed because she *felt* things. (Quill knew she existed because she *saw* things.) Meg was feeling a lot of very intense, contrary emotions. So there was an internal logic here. The logic just wasn't clear at the moment. Quill just hoped Meg figured it out before she married Andy Bishop.

Tom set a double martini with two onions in front of Quill. Which made it a Gibson, not a martini, and Quill didn't want it anyway. Meg noticed, of course, and scribbled another note. He served Doreen her drink, and then set a plate in the center of the table. "The chef's compliments, ladies. This evening's *amusée bouche.*"

"Bless you!" Doreen said, and knocked back a second slug of her drink.

Meg leaned forward and stared at the hors d'ouevres disapprovingly.

"And your wine, miss." He displayed the bottle with a flourish. "The '97? Yes?" He uncorked it (not without a struggle) and poured a glass for both Dina and Meg. He bowed and left.

Meg sipped the wine, rolled it around in her mouth, swallowed, and scribbled furiously.

"Now, Meg," Quill protested. "It was a plastic cork. Our waiters have trouble with plastic corks. And with a plastic cork the wine never gets, well, corked. So there wasn't any need to have you test it first."

"Tradition," Meg scowled. "It could have fermented, couldn't it? And we had a training session with the waitstaff about the plastic corks. Jerry should have done that, too."

"Is this really a good idea?" Quill asked. "Is this really fair? I was looking forward to eating at Elise's. And I was the one who invited you all out to dinncr. I should have picked the restaurant."

Meg looked at Quill over the rim of her spectacles. "Do you know what happened when I went down to make sure Jerry was ready to handle my kitchen?" Her tone was sweetly reasonable.

"What?"

"He'd taken Duck Quilliam off the menu."

"Oh." Quill took a long sip of the Gibson. "My goodness."

"Do you know why?"

"Not a clue." She looked at Doreen. Doreen shook her head in warning. Quill took another long sip of the Gibson. She had a good hunch about why Jerry'd taken Duck Quilliam off the menu. Duck Quilliam wasn't very good. Duck, Meg said, was a challenge to any artist in the kitchen. It was a challenge she could handle. Like all artists, Meg could dig her heels in. And she'd dug her heels in about Duck Quilliam. The fact that the dish was returned to the kitchen half-eaten more often than not was proof to Meg that the palate of the average American diner was in need of education.

Meg leaned forward and hissed, "He said the mushroom stuffing fought with the cranberry compote, which in turn fought with the black bean risotto. And that it all smothered the duck."

"Goodness," Doreen said sympathetically. "I think your duck's pretty near the best I ever had."

Jerry was right. And Doreen knew perfectly well Jerry was right. Quill drank the rest of the Gibson. "And what did you say?" she asked Meg, against her better judgment.

"I said 'we'll see about that, Jerry Grimsby'." Meg tapped her notebook. She smiled in a chilling way. "And here I am. Seeing about it."

"And then," Quill said to Myles some hours later, "she ordered the duck."

"She ordered the duck?"

"Yep." Quill lay flat on her back on her couch and stared up at the ceiling. Myles sat in the Eames chair, his feet up on the hassock, the *Syracuse Herald* on his lap. It was just after eleven o'clock. "Duck Grimsby."

"And?"

Quill rolled over on her side so she could see him better. "It was great. I tried some. The skin was crisp, the duck was moist and whatever Jerry did with the apple chutney was incredible. It made Meg so mad she sent it back to the kitchen. She told Tom the waiter it was inedible."

Myles shook his head in commiseration. "So then what?"

"Then we came back here and ran into three of the Boom-Boom girls." Quill frowned at the heap of clothes on the floor. "Taffi and Candi thought my wig was the funniest thing they'd ever seen. They hooted up a storm. Meg got huffy, because she was feeling stupid, so she threw her wig and the spectacles at them and stalked off and I had to apologize, which I did, handsomely, if I may say so. Partly because it was rude of Meg, but mostly because I shouldn't have had that second Gibson."

"And then?

Myles really was the most incredibly patient man. Quill smiled lovingly at him. "Now she's in her room across the hall. Writing the review. And she's *wearing bile-green socks*."

Myles smiled a little. Then he picked up the middle section of the newspaper and started to do the crossword. Quill rolled on her back and stared at the ceiling again. Her head ached slightly. It was either the second Gibson or not enough sleep. "I'm worried about her."

"She'll be fine."

"You never knew her husband, Daniel. I've told you about Daniel."

"I remember."

"They'd only been married a year when he was killed in that car accident. He was a stockbroker. He was a great guy, Myles. Steady, calm, terrific future. It was perfect. Just perfect. And then it blew apart. Just like that. I've been so afraid that life wouldn't give her a second chance, but it has. Andy's wonderful. Just as steady, just as calm as Daniel, and look at how successful he is. The clinic's grown by leaps. Leaps. Did you know he has patients coming in from Syracuse and Rochester just to see him? It's a fact. Well. There it is." She sat up, suddenly. "Do you want a glass of wine before we go to bed? Myles?"

Myles had set the paper down and was looking at her. "You have the most peculiar expression on your face. What is it?"

"Is that what Meg wants? Steady, calm, successful?"

"Of course it's what she wants! You know how volatile she is."

"And is that what you want? Steady, calm, successful?"

"That's different." Quill smiled at him. "I like dangerous, brave, and adventuresome."

He stood up, then came over and sat next to her, his arm around her shoulder, his face in her hair. "Glad to hear it."

She leaned back, the better to see his face. "Are you sure you're okay?"

"I'm fine. It's you I'm concerned about."

"The only thing I'm concerned about is getting some sleep."

"That's better than being concerned about Meg. Or Antonia Caprese."

"Who? Oh." Quill waved her hand airily. "You mean the small-time hood whose body was found in MacAvoy's barn?"

"That Antonia Caprese, Quill. Yes." His grip tightened to a brief hug. He released her and he got to his feet.

Quill yawned. "I told you. I'm not going to ask you a thing about her."

Myles looked down at her. "Yeah. You did."

"So?" Quill gave him an innocent smile.

"So will you give me your word to stay out of this one?"

"This case, you mean."

"That's the one I mean. It's a nasty one, and I don't want you near it."

Quill wriggled her eyebrows at him. "You mean . . . the Mob?"

Myles looked particularly impassive when he'd felt she'd gone too far.

Quill apologized. Then she tugged at her lower lip. "Tell you what. I give you my word not to interfere with any police investigation. And I also promise to deliver any information I stumble across . . ."

"Stumble across!"

"Or that falls in my lap. Or that I overhear accidentally. Anything like that. I'll tell you like this." She snapped her fingers. "Instantly. This is me, on the cell phone, calling you, Myles." She leaned forward and rapped her knuckles on her oak chest. "Hello? Hello? Is this the sheriff?"

"Is this the sheriff? Is this the sheriff?" The scream, a feminine one, was accompanied by a frantic thumping on Quill's front door. "Are you in there? Help! Help!"

Myles was across the room in two seconds flat. Quill was right behind him. He flung open the door and Brittney-Anne fell into Myles' arms, her face wet with tears. "He's dead!" she shrieked. "Leo's dead!"

Myles grasped her firmly by the shoulders. "Where is he?"

Brittney-Anne threw her head back and shrieked. Myles put his hand under her chin and looked her firmly in the eye. Brittney-Anne flung her arms around his neck in a stranglehold and collapsed against his chest.

Quill whirled into her small kitchen, pulled a pitcher of ice water from the undercounter fridge and dampened a clean dish towel. She walked back to the screaming stripper and gripped Myles' forearm. "Let me."

He backed away. She put her arms around Brittney-Anne, led her to the couch and settled her down. She applied the cold cloth to Brittney-Anne's face. The shrieks stopped abruptly and Brittney-Anne snatched the cloth from Quill's hands.

"That's cold, dammit!"

"You must tell us where Leo is," Quill said gently.

"And you smeared my makeup," Brittney-Anne scowled.

Quill looked at her thoughtfully. Myles, a rare impatience in his voice, asked her again.

"Your goddam parking lot, that's where. Why you don't have more lights out there?"

Myles was out the door before she finished, his cell phone in his hand. Quill raced after him, down the steps, out the front door, and around the east end of the building to the guest parking lot. Before either of them reached it, sirens sounded in the distance. Davy must have already been in the patrol car, Quill thought, and oh, god, there was the siren for the ambulance, too, and they probably should have more lights in the lot. What if Leo had been murdered? What if someone backed over him because they couldn't see him in the dark?

They both saw Leo at the same time, under the perfectly adequate halogen lamp that lit the south end of the lot, and he wasn't dead. He was leaning against his Cadillac. He was bloody. And cursing a blue streak. And Jerry Grimsby was with him.

CHAPTER 8

"Well, that puts the kibosh on Maltby as the perp," Doreen said with relish. "Unless there's two murderers running around here. Or unless Maltby beat up his ownself." She looked pleased at the prospect.

"Nobody else has been murdered," Quill said crossly. "And Maltby was mugged. That's all there is to it."

Doreen sniffed in disparagement. Whether the disparagement was for the mugger or Maltby, Quill couldn't say.

Doreen sat next to Dina on the couch in Quill's office. Dina was dressed in her usual work outfit, black pants with a white tee shirt with the Inn logo on it. She clutched a thin stack of paper. Doreen was dressed in what she referred to as her Sunday-go-to-meetin' garb: a beige polyester pantsuit and a flowered blouse.

It was seven o'clock in the morning. Dina and Doreen had dragged Quill out of bed at the unconscionable hour of six o'clock, demanding a meeting. She'd sent them downstairs to her office, swallowed three cups of extra-dark Espresso, and then stood under a cold shower. It hadn't helped. Quill could hardly keep her eyes open. All she wanted to do was put her head down on her desk and sleep.

With a semblance of alertness, Quill said, "He's not dead, Doreen. Just roughed up a little bit. And I still think he had something to do with the body in MacAvoy's barn. But you know what? I don't care if he did. I don't care who beat him up, either. And if this meeting is about solving who did either of those things, forget it. I'm out of the detective business. I never get any sleep when I'm in the detective business. So this meeting better be about whose handling the housekeeping duties, Doreen. And Dina, you don't need to be here at all."

Dina (surprisingly) didn't take umbrage at this surly comment. "Of course I need to be here. Look what happens when I'm not! All kinds of stuff. I can't believe that I missed everything last night. I shouldn't have stayed over at Davy's. I should have come back here with you guys. A mugging in Hemlock Falls!"

Quill was very fond of Dina. Most of the time. But not at the moment. "It was horrible," she said coldly. "I would have been delighted to miss it."

"You've got a hangover," Dina said sympathetically. "Those Gibsons you drank last night would give anybody a hangover. Want some aspirin?"

"I am not hungover. I'm sleep-deprived." She looked blearily out her office window. It was going to be another hot, sunny August day, although it was hazy. She went to the window and looked to the northwest. A thin line of dark clouds intimated rain later. She hoped it rained hard. She hoped it rained so hard that the gorge backed up, overflowed and washed the entire Inn downriver to Mississippi with all its occupants in it. Then she could get some sleep.

"Grouchy," Doreen said to Dina. "You know what I think? I think she's still steamed about pretendin' to be Meg's ma."

"I am not," Quill said indignantly. "If I'm steamed about anything it's that stupid wig."

"Uh-huh. So, do we have two criminals, or do you think Maltby beat up his ownself?" Doreen offered this again in a diversionary spirit.

"Of course I don't think Maltby beat himself up." Quill sat down behind her desk again and regarded her housekeeper crossly. Except Doreen wasn't her housekeeper anymore; she was the self-appointed travel tour director of the Inn at Hemlock Falls. Which was probably why she was dressed up in her pantsuit. There'd been no chance to discuss this during the debacle at Seasons in the Sun the night before. Quill admitted to herself that she didn't want to discuss it now, either. "Why am I up this early?"

"She's not grouchy," Doreen amended. "She's pitiful."

She did sound pitiful. She hated sounding pitiful. She'd looked in on Meg before she'd come downstairs to find her sister peacefully zonked out on her couch, surrounded by wadded up drafts of her restaurant review. Why couldn't she be zonked out, too?

"Well, you asked for our help on this case," Dina said cheerfully. "Here we are to give it. I've got info. I figured you'd want it right away. Especially since things seem to be escalating."

"I didn't ask for your help on this case. You volunteered."

"Back to grouchy," Doreen observed.

"Fine. I'm grouchy, pitiful, and sleep-deprived. I've changed my mind. We aren't detecting anymore. We've got an Inn to run. Not to mention Meg's wedding." Quill said this very firmly. Then she added, "You have some new information? About the body?"

Dina nodded. "Yep. I Googled Antonia Caprese. Then I Googled Mr. Maltby." She leaned forward with a conspiratal air. "Where is Mr. Maltby right now, anyway?"

Quill sighed. "He's barricaded himself in his suite upstairs. I took him down to the emergency room last night. He has a concussion and a couple of impressive bruises. Allie Williams stitched him up and wanted to keep him overnight for observation, but he flatly refused. He insisted on coming back here." She stared up at the ceiling, feeling baleful. "Norrie Ferguson is sitting right outside the door. I hope he doesn't have a gun. It would be just like that guy to sit there with a gun."

"Aren't you going to go up and check on him and Brittney-Anne?" Dina asked cheerfully.

"*She's* doing just fine." Quill set her cup of coffee down on her desk with a little more sharpness than she'd intended. Last night, Brittney-Anne had flung herself into Myles' arms. Repeatedly. She'd yelled 'Dead! Dead! Dead!' All the way into the parking lot. Brittney-Anne had created enough noise to wake the dead, but of course, all she'd done was wake up half the guests, most of whom would probably check out this morning. She'd distinctly heard the elderly couple in 122 refer to the Inn as Murder Motel.

She wasn't convinced that Brittney-Anne had thought Leo was dead, either. She was simply being hysterical. When Quill and Myles had gotten down to the parking lot, Leo was standing up cursing a blue streak. He had looked pretty horrible with all that blood streaming down his face, but he was very far from looking like a corpse.

"Did Brittney-Anne see who done it?" Doreen pulled a little steno book from the big black purse she carried everywhere. "Stoke asked me to get the partic'lars. He's down to the office writing the story right now.

'Crime wave in Hemlock Falls,' " she continued with relish. " 'Citizens Alert.' I'm going to call it in, soon as I finish getting all the facts." She, too, gazed up at the ceiling. "I'll be doin' an interview with Brittney-Anne of course. I should prob'ly interview you, too, Quill. Seeing as how you were practically an eyewitness."

Quill closed her eyes and put her head down on her desk. She didn't want to get into yet another discussion about freedom of the press with Doreen. She didn't want to be interviewed, either. Myles had taken a brief statement from Leo and Brittney-Anne and disappeared. She hadn't seen him since. She'd gotten to bed at two o'clock after bringing Leo back from the hospital and been dragged out of bed at six. Now all she wanted was to go upstairs and take a nap. She sat up and scrubbed at her face with both hands. "I don't think you'll get much out of either of them, Doreen. All Brittney-Anne said was that they'd gone to visit some friends in Syracuse. They got back around eleven. Leo parked that whacking big Lincoln he drives. They both got out. Leo got a call on his cell phone. Brittney-Anne left him to it—actually, she said he told her to beat it—and she walked on ahead to the Inn. Leo shouted—she couldn't remember what, apparently, and she heard the sound of something being slammed against the car. She didn't look back, she just ran to the nearest door, which happened to be the kitchen, and grabbed Jerry Grimsby." Trust Brittney-Anne to throw herself at the nearest good-looking male. "Jerry sent her on up to Myles and ran out to the parking lot. By the time we got there, there wasn't anything to see. So I'm not an eyewitness. I'm an innocent bystander."

Doreen scribbled assiduously in her notebook. "Then Leo musta seen who done it."

"If he did, he's not saying a word."

"Hm." Doreen scrawled one more line and closed the notebooks with a flourish. "I'll just take the camera and go on up there. Still got a lot of blood on him, has he?"

"Not a speck. It all got washed off at the clinic. And if I were you, Doreen, I'd think twice about tackling Mr. Maltby. He's not in the best of tempers at the moment. And if he refused to talk to Myles, why should he talk to you?"

"Quill's absolutely right," Dina said. "If we're going to get any information about this case, we'll just have to sneak around like every other detective on the job."

Quill wished (not for the first time) that she wore spectacles. If she wore spectacles, she could gaze over them in an intimidating way. "We are not detectives on the job. We are employees of this Inn on the job."

Dina and Doreen exchanged glances. "So you don't want to see what I dug up on Antonia Caprese?" Dina said innocently. "Or Mr. Maltby?" She held up her stack of papers.

Quill was torn. She really was. She thought about it for a minute, then shook her head. "No. Myles is right. We shouldn't be poking around in this mess. Whoever smacked Leo Maltby around could smack us around, too. This is getting dangerous. I want you, Dina, to handle reception. Don't let any reporters in. Don't talk to anyone in the media. If the other guests are anxious about what happened. . . ." Quill waved her hands helplessly. "I don't know. Tell them we are very, very sorry about the disturbance, but we're sure this has to do with a private matter between Mr. Maltby and some friends of his."

Dina looked dubious. Then she thumbed through the sheaf of printouts in her hand. She stopped to read a few lines, raised her eyebrows and clicked her tongue disapprovingly. Then she said, "Wow!" She tapped the printouts into a neat stack and stuffed them in her tote bag. "Okay. You're the boss!" She hopped off the couch and started out the door.

"But you might . . ." Quill said.

Dina looked back.

"Just leave the papers here. For a bit."

"You mean this really interesting stuff from Google? These papers?"

Quill made a face.

"So we are in the detect—"

"Out," Quill said. "And please please please don't let anyone check out if you can possibly avoid it."

"This is me, headed out to defend the perimeter." Dina dropped the papers on Quill's desk, gave Doreen a high sign, and shut the office door behind her with a happy bang.

Quill sat back with a sigh.

"You really think people'll want to leave?" Doreen asked.

"I'm afraid so." Quill ran her hands through her hair.

"I thought we were going to have a good quarter, but now I'm not so sure."

"Leave it to me," Doreen said confidently. "This here job of travel director ain't hard at all. First day on the job, heck, first afternoon on the job, I got us three suites booked just like that."

"You did," Quill said warmly. "But gosh, Doreen, don't you think Taffi and Candi and Sheree . . ." she trailed off. She didn't have the guts to pick her way through this particular minefield. She just hadn't thought through her principles yet, that was the problem.

"Nice girls," Doreen said affably. "You know, they had some problems at the Marriott down on Route 15."

"They did?" Quill sat up, indignant. "You mean they wouldn't let them have rooms? Just because of the way they dress?"

"Nah. They had rooms all right. Thing is, Taffi said the management mistook the friendly way they were talkin' to some guys in the bar." Doreen folded her hands on her lap with a demure air.

"Oh." Quill swallowed and took the bull by the horns. "Friendly in what way, do you think?"

Doreen's beady black eyes twinkled. "Well, you know. Overfriendly, like."

"Oh, dear."

"But I wouldn't worry. That there Sheree pitched a fit."

"At Gully Anderson?" Gully, the amiable manager of the Marriott, handled fits of any description with aplomb. He was an easygoing guy, as wcll.

"Nope. Not at Gully. At Taffi and Candi."

Quill cocked her head interrogatively.

"That Sheree's got her head on straight," Doreen said. "What I mean to say is, I wouldn't worry about the girls. If you know what I mean."

"I think I know what you mean," Quill said cautiously. "Sheree said it's kind of a mission with her, seein' that the girls keep on the right side of friendly."

"So they aren't . . ."

"Not so's you notice."

"And they aren't being exploited? I mean really, Doreen, the poor things . . ." Quill reflected a moment. "This is what bothers me. Women who don't have a choice. Especially if there are drugs in the picture. That's bad, Doreen. It's awful. And it's not fair."

Doreen snorted. "You think I been runnin' the housekeepin' staff and takin' care of guests for ten years without knowing how and when to look for trouble?"

Quill looked at her. She hadn't thought about it. But when she did think about it she wanted to smack herself on the side of the head. Of course Doreen knew what she was doing. A couple of incidents came to mind almost immediately. The dangerously slick guy from New York, who'd complained about the cleaning job in his room, and then left abruptly. The two pallid women filmmakers from LA who'd scarpered in the middle of the night without paying the bill. The amazingly meek behavior of the over-the-hill rock star who'd left 330 in such a mess. Quill found herself with an increasing respect for Doreen's sharp eye. And her mop. "Do you think Kathleen's up to the job?"

"Wouldn't a suggested her if I didn't," Doreen said tartly. "But I'm keepin' my hand in with her. We had a talk yesterday and we'll talk more before it's over."

"So about this job of travel director?"

"Ay-uh."

"You think you'll be comfortable with it?"

Doreen smiled at her. There was a lot of affection in that smile, and a lot of wisdom, and Quill got up and kissed the top of her head, thinking how lucky she was to have Doreen and Dina and Meg and the whole lot of them, even though they drove her crazy every half minute.

"Go on with you," Doreen said roughly. "Now are you gonna let me interview Leo Maltby, or are you gonna pitch a fit? I promised Stoke a story before my next birthday."

"I'm not going to pitch a fit," Quill promised. "But I'll go up with you. I want to see how he's doing. And for goodness sake, Doreen, don't ask him to unwrap his bandages or anything, will you?"

"Photo op," Doreen said regretfully.

"Forget it."

On her way up the three flights of stairs to Leo's suite, Quill started worrying that Norrie Ferguson was sitting outside his partner's suite with a gun in his pocket. She had no reason to suspect that either Leo or Norrie carried guns, other than the nature of Leo's business interests. And the fact that the body of a small-time hood had been found on a piece of property purchased by Lovejoy Enterprises. Not to mention that someone had tried his best to rearrange Leo's nose around his socks last night in her parking lot. Which gave her a lot of reasons to worry about guns. Quill didn't like guns. In her opinion, the only people who should have guns were the police.

But Norrie Ferguson wasn't sitting outside suite 321 with or without a gun. He was inside the suite with Taffi, Candi, Sheree, and Leo himself. They were playing poker.

321 was the Provençal suite, and it was one of Quill's favorite rooms. The dominant colors were blue and yellow, with accents of green and tangerine. A white-brick fireplace with a carved mantel dominated the small living room. French doors led out onto a balcony overlooking the sweep of the Falls. The climbing rose blaze twined around the balustrade. The doors were open to the soft summer air, and the scent of roses collided with the smell of Leo's cigar. Someone had drawn the small Louis Quatorze dining table over to the couch, where Leo lay half-upright, a can of beer in one hand and his cigar in the other.

Leo was subdued. The pouches under his eyes were black edged with blue. The fringe of hair around his bald head had been shaved on one side, and a large square bandage covered his left temple. His right cheek was scraped raw from the gravel on the surface of the parking lot. Quill winced in spite of herself. He'd looked a lot worse last night, but there hadn't been time for wincing then.

"Hey, cookie," he greeted her. He stuck the cigar between his teeth. His cockiness came with an effort and his eyes were dull.

"How are you feeling, Mr. Maltby?"

He shrugged. " 'Bout time you called me Leo, innit? Seein's as how I bled all over your skirt last night." His teeth flashed in a momentary grin. "It was a whatdya-callit. Bonding experience."

Sheree put down her poker hand and got up. "Hey, Quill. We want to thank you for taking Leo down to the hospital last night." Her blonde hair was drawn back in a neat ponytail. She was wearing cut-off jeans and a baggy tee-shirt. The sunlight cascading into the room was bright and Quill could see the tired lines in her face under the heavy makeup.

"He probably should have stayed overnight," Quill said frankly.

"Ah, I'm tough as old boot. Four queens." Leo said, and laid his hand down with a flourish. "See? Take a lot more'n a few thumps to topple the Boom."

"Lee-oh!" Taffi said. She pouted and threw her hand across the table. She was dressed in a pink negligee with a lot of rabbit fur at the wrists and neck.

"Tell you girls what," Leo said. "Take the pot and go down and get some breakfast, or take a walk or something."

"A walk?" Candi wrinkled her smooth brow. She had on a skimpy halter top and a pair of satin pajama bottoms.

"Yeah. Get some fresh air. Whatever."

"There are some very nice shops in the village," Quill said. "And if you stop at the desk, Dina will give you a map. We have a van and a driver available if you'd like to tour the wineries or visit some of the surrounding gorges."

Taffi shrugged and gathered the considerable number of bills on the table into her lap.

"Good idea, girls." Sheree nudged Taffi out of the chair. "Get changed, both of you. Jeans and tee-shirts, okay? We don't want to drive the natives crazy. Just be back here in time for rehearsal, 'kay? Two o'clock." She raised her voice as they edged around Doreen and Quill to get to the door. "And stay out of trouble. Got it?"

Taffi didn't look back, but waved one languid hand in farewell.

"Hang on a sec, guys." Sheree looked anxiously at Leo. "You know what, Boom? I think, like, I should go with them. You sure you're gonna be okay here?"

Norrie Ferguson cleared his throat meaningfully and patted his waist. He was wearing another Hawaiian shirt. This one belled voluminously over his white sharkskin pants. Quill bit her lip nervously. Was that a gun-shaped bulge over his back pocket?

"I got Norrie to get stuff for me if I need anything. And Brittney-Anne'll look after me," Leo said. His gaze wandered to the bedroom door, which was firmly closed. "If she ever gets that cute little butt out of bed," he added. Quill thought he didn't sound all that elated at the prospect. "Plus, this place is growin' on me, Sher.

I'm thinking of settling down here. So go on ahead. I'm fine. Besides, those two'll have the pants off half the guys in town if you don't ride herd on 'em. Just get 'em back here in time for the rehearsal this afternoon."

"Is there anything we can get for you, Leo?" Quill asked politely.

"Nah. Room service is pretty good here." He waved the beer in her direction.

"There is something," Sheree said. "What about the rehearsal rooms? Can you recommend a place in town, Quill?"

"Wait a minute, wait a minute. Lemme think." Leo chomped heavily on his cigar. You rent out rooms, right?"

"Yes, we do," Quill said cordially. "But I'm afraid that we don't have enough room to help you interview any prospective dancers. I've already discussed this a bit with Sheree, and she said your ads pull hundreds of prospectve employees in and we really don't have . . ."

"I ain't runnin' those ads just yet. I'm savin' that up. I mean like the girls I got gotta have a place to rehearse."

"The girls you got gotta . . . oh! You mean rehearse?"

Leo chuckled, a mere ghost of his former ebullient roar. "You don't think they keep those bods by guzzling beer and chips and sittin' around on those cute butts all day? We need a big place with enough room for Sher here to put 'em through their paces. You rent out that bar of yours?"

"The Tavern Lounge?"

"Sure we do," Doreen interjected, "but it'll cost ya. Big time."

Leo waved the cigar. "No sweat there. Put it on the tab. You'll need what, Sher, a couple of hours?" He squinted at Quill in a friendly way.

"At least, Boom," Sheree said.

Doreen made a note in her little book. "Two to four okay?" she asked briskly. "That's peak time here, Maltby. If we close the Lounge, it'll cost ya a thousand bucks, easy. Maybe two."

Quill felt dizzy. Leo's smile became a little less friendly. He addressed Quill with a snap. "So who is this dame when she's at home?"

"Dame?" Quill said, "You mean Doreen? I mean, Ms. Muxworthy-Stoker?"

"My job is travel director," Doreen said. She glared at Leo, who shrank back a bit. "I handle events, too," she said to Quill. "I been meanin' to give you the job description." She swiveled her beady gaze back to the couch. "You got it, Maltby. Tavern Bar's yours from two to four this afternoon."

"Thanks, Dorie." Sheree gave Doreen's arm an appreciative squeeze.

"No sweat, Sher."

"We'll be off now, Boom. See you in a bit."

Dorie? Quill kept her smile firmly in place as Sheree followed her two charges out the door. "Well," she began, aware of the somewhat dazed cheer in her voice. "The hospital did say they'd like to see you again today, Leo . . ."

"Thought maybe I could get an interview before you went and got yourself looked at," Doreen elbowed her way past Quill and planted herself in the chair Sheree had vacated. "For the *Gazette.*"

Leo's somewhat vacant gaze brightened. "Local rag?" he guessed. "You betcha." He straightened himself with an effort. "You need a press kit? Norrie, get her a press kit."

"You sent one of them down to the *Gazette*. What I wanta know is what happened last night." Doreen settled a pair of horn-rimmed glasses on her nose and peered at her notebook. "What happened? Who hit you? Where," she broke off to scribble, "parking lot, that I got." She resumed with a deep breath. "How was you hit?"

"What the hell?" Leo said in confusion. "Wait a minit. I thought you were the whadyacallit. Travel director. I thought this was about publicity."

"And investigative reporter," Doreen said. "I guess you could call me a multitasker."

"Why don't you report on this, then? Lovejoy's Nudie Bar and Grill will be the classiest strip joint in a hundred miles of this hick town."

"That I got," Doreen said. "That was in the press kit. What I wanna know is who thumped you?"

Leo's eyes shifted from left to right. "I dunno who thumped me. Who cares who thumped me?"

"You don't care who umm . . . thumped you?" Quill said, startled out of a reluctant silence.

Leo sucked his bottom lip. "I wouldn't say as I don't

care," he said craftily. "Can't see how it's anybody's business but mine, though."

"You musta seen something," Doreen urged.

Leo took his cigar out of his mouth and regarded it with a thoughtful air. "Nope."

"Nope?" Quill echoed. "The lot's very well-lighted, Leo. You must have seen *something*."

"Musta snuck up behind me." He wiggled his eyebrows at Doreen. "So. How's about if I arrange for a few photo ops with the Boom-Boom girls for this *Gazette*? Get 'em all tricked out in a few costumes. It'd make a heck of a front page spread."

Quill tugged thoughtfully at her lower lip. Leo was treating his assault in a very cavalier way. Although she supposed that the last thing a murderer wanted was more attention from the police. But if the last thing Leo wanted was more attention from the police, why was he so anxious for more publicity for Lovejoy's Nudie Bar and Grill when more publicity would just mean another visit by the placard-carrying members of Women Against Crimes Against Women? And this time she herself would call the cops.

There was a lot that didn't add up here. Suddenly, she was very eager to take a look at what Dina had found on the Internet about Antonia Caprese. The clue to this case had to be found in the victim's past. Every amateur detective worth her salt knew that. "I have been neglecting the prime imperative of every investigation," Quill said aloud.

"Say what?" Leo asked.

"This story I'm writing here's about the mugging!" Doreen said loudly. "We never had a mugging in Hemlock Falls before."

"We must have," Quill said.

"We have not."

"Muggings are pandemic," Quill said. "Hemlock Falls is no exception."

"Who mugged 'im, then?"

"I don't know," Quill admitted.

"I'll tell you who. It's not anybody from around here, I'll tell you that. It's gotta be somebody attached to that there resort Mr. High and Mighty Rodman's set up, that's who."

"Here, now," Maltby said. "If those are the guys that run me out of the press conference I can tell you right now, it wasn't any of them."

"No?" Quill said with interest. "So you *do* know who hit you?"

Maltby threw his hands in the air. "Jeez!" he said. "Can't a guy just get a little peace?"

"Just a little bit more," Doreen said encouragingly. "What I want to know is what happened and why you think somebody conked you over the head. You tell me that, I'll talk to Stoke about tannin' them pictures of the Boom-Boom girls in the paper."

"Who gives a rat's behind about a little whack on the bean?" Leo asked the ceiling.

"Our readers, that's who."

Quill sighed. This could go on all day.

The bedroom door opened. Brittney-Anne stuck her

head into the living room. She was in full makeup. Quill wondered if she slept in it. The sunlight, which had been so harsh on Sheree's features, only served to make Brittney-Anne more beautiful. "Would you all just flippin' shut up out here?"

"Hey, Brittney," Leo said warily. "Just a little press conference. Why don't you haul your behind out here and give us an interview?"

"Flip off, Leo. I need coffee. *Now.*" She slammed the door shut again.

"Norrie?" Leo said.

"You stay right there, Mr. Ferguson. I'll see to it." Grateful for the reprieve, Quill headed to the door and was out in the hall before anyone could protest, if anyone was going to protest, which she doubted. Both Doreen and Leo were equally matched. And Norrie Ferguson seemed content to sit and stare at nothing in particular. She glanced at her watch. It was a few minutes after eight. How could it be only be a few minutes after eight in the morning? She leaned against the wall for a moment and closed her eyes. Here's what she could do. She could go to her rooms, call down for coffee for Brittney-Anne, and go back to bed. Just for an hour. Everybody at the Chamber of Commerce was mad at her, so she wasn't going to be called into any emergency meetings. Myles was goodness knew where. Dina was perfectly capable of handling any inquiries at the front desk. Except she hadn't been down to the kitchen yet, nor had she checked on how breakfast was going. And she really should talk to Kathleen and see how the whole housekeeping thing was coming.

"And on top of that," she said aloud, "where's that darn dog?" She really was letting things get out of hand.

"Max? Investigating the Dumpster at the Croh Bar."

Quill's eyes flew open. "Andy?"

"That's the last I saw of him," Andy Bishop said. He walked toward her. He'd clearly come from the far end of the hall, where Meg and Quill both had their rooms. He was carrying a black bag.

Quill looked at him anxiously. "You looked tired." Actually, Andy always looked a little tired. He was a little taller than Quill herself, a slender, well-knit man with fair hair and pleasant blue eyes. He wasn't a particularly expressive man—a reassuring trait in a physician, as far as Quill was concerned. She indicated the bag with a smile. "Are you making a house call?"

"Thought I'd check up on Mr. Maltby, yes." His smile was brief. "You look a little tired yourself."

"Well, Meg probably told you about last night." She looked past him to Meg's door. It was closed.

"I heard about it at the clinic," he said obliquely. "I hope the emergency room staff acquitted themselves well?"

"They did."

"Well. Meg didn't say much to me about it. She seems to have missed a lot of it."

"She could sleep through a barrage in Beirut," Quill said, although, now that she thought about it, it was odd that she hadn't seen her sister at all last night. The rumpus that Britnney-Anne made would have aroused the denizens of the Civil War cemetery half a mile away, much less her little sister.

Andy touched her arm lightly. "Excuse me. I take it Leo's in?"

Quill moved away from the door to Leo's suite. "Yes. Yes. He doesn't look as if he'll be going anywhere today."

Andy knocked, then went inside after a muffled shout of "it's open." Quill stared at the closed door for a long moment, then marched briskly to her sister's door.

Which was locked.

Quill tapped.

"Beat it!" Meg yelled.

"It's me, Meggie."

"I know who it is. I said beat it!"

"How could you know who it is? The door's shut!"

Meg flung the door open. Her face was red. She was in her nightshirt, the one with the duck on the front with the legend that read: I'M BAD. "I knew who it was because only you tap like that." She slammed the door shut in Quill's face.

Quill tugged at her lower lip, then tapped at the door again. "Jerry sent me. There's a problem in the kitchen."

"You're just trying to get in here. The kitchen's fine!"

"But Jerry said . . ."

Meg flung the door open again. "Yeah? Jerry said what?"

"That there's a problem in the kitchen," Quill said

brightly. "I don't know. He could have solved it by now. But maybe we should go and check it out."

Meg turned and said over her shoulder. "Jerry? Is there a problem in the kitchen?" She turned back to Quill, smiling sweetly. "He says no. And how would he know anyway? He hasn't been near the kitchen all night."

She shut the door. Gently.

CHAPTER 9

"Oh my gosh." Dina stood up behind the reception desk as Quill entered the foyer. "What happened?"

Quill wasn't aware that she'd walked all the way down three flights of stairs. She blinked at Dina. "What are you doing here?"

"I work here."

Quill made a noise.

"Whoa," Dina said.

" 'Whoa' what?"

"You snarled. You never snarl."

Quill made the noise again.

Dina sat down again, rather tentatively. "You're not going to throw anything, are you?"

"What!?"

"Nothing," Dina said hastily, "I didn't say a word. These lips are sealed. Forget I'm even here." She moved the stapler out of sight and put the telephone on the floor beside her chair. Quill looked at the reception desk, which was now clear of throwable objects. Too bad. "Did you need to see me?"

"Actually," Dina said. "You came to see me. Or at least, you came down the stairs. And I'm at the end of them."

Quill looked back at the stairs. So she had. "Things are out of control. Have you noticed that things are out of control?"

"Nope. All I've noticed are a couple of phone calls that you should probably return. I can put them in your office if you'd like. And maybe get you a cup of tea." Her voice rose. "Where are you going?"

Quill had just decided what to do. She'd been so mad that she hadn't been able to decide what to do, but now things were crystal clear. "The kitchen."

Dina edged out onto the oriental rug that covered the main part of the foyer and grabbed Quill's arm. "Take a couple of deep breaths. Think cheerful thoughts."

Quill breathed. Then she looked at the rug. She liked the rug, although it wasn't really a practical choice for an entrance area. The background was cream, overwoven with flowers in celadon, pink, sage, and peach. She stared at it for a long moment.

"I think you should, like, maybe sit in the office for a sec," Dina said. "Just 'til you calm down a bit more."

"I am perfectly calm. I'll be even calmer after I get to the kitchen."

"Why?"

"I am going to the kitchen to get the ten-inch boning knife. And I am going out to the parking lot and puncture all the tires on Jerry Grimsby's truck. And then I am going back upstairs and puncture Jerry Grimsby.”

“Whoa,” Dina said.

“You are repeating yourself,” Quill said icily.

“You might want to think about whether or not you want to puncture Jerry. Who’s going to run the kitchen while Meg gets married?” Dina leaped a little at the expression on Quill’s face. “Well. Okay then. You won’t have to go back upstairs to puncture Jerry Grimsby if you’re that determined to do it. He’s in the kitchen.”

“He is not. He is . . .” Quill clamped her mouth shut. Upstairs with my crazy sister! “Not in the kitchen.”

“He was like, in the kitchen thirty seconds ago. He’s been there all morning.”

“How do you know that?” Quill demanded.

Dina shrugged. “He just called me on the intercom and asked if I wanted some cinnamon focaccia. I said sure. I love cinnamon foccacia. And Quill, Meg never asks me if I’d like cinnamon foccacia or anything else. Jerry’s really nice about stuff like that. And here he is. Hi, Jer.”

Quill whirled. It was indeed Jerry Grimsby, coming through the dining room, a basket in one hand and a cup of cappuccino in the other. His chef’s coat was open and he was wearing a dark blue shirt that read: I’M TOO SEXY FOR MY HAIR. Quill grabbed the front of his shirt and twisted it. The cappuccino bounced off the oak floor. The basket of foccacia hit one of the two tall oriental vases that stood in front of the reception desk. Jerry went “urk” then said mildly, “Hey!”

Quill released him, pulled open her office door and said furiously. "In here."

Once in her office, she pushed him onto the couch and stood over him, her hands on her hips. "Have you no shame?"

Jerry appeared to consider this. "Very little," he said, in an agreeable way. "And not a lot of guilt, either. Should I?"

He didn't look like a man who had been making love to her sister just five minutes ago. He looked like a man who'd been putting the finishing touches on the cinnamon focaccia that was all over the floor in the foyer. There was cinnamon on his nose.

"Where were you this morning?" Quill demanded.

"Where was I? In the kitchen."

"And where were you last night?"

"I had a late-night TV interview with Angela Stoner. Channel 15 put me up in the Hilton. Breakfast was disgusting."

"You had a talk show interview?"

His face fell. "You didn't see it. I thought everybody knew about it. Did Meg see it?"

"Did she?" Quill asked coolly.

Jerry gave her a wary glance. "What's up?"

"When did you last see Meg?"

"Yesterday afternoon when we all came back to the Inn from the Croh Bar. I thought she was going to come into the kitchen and talk about the night's menu, but she never showed up. Well, actually, Bjarne told me she did get to the kitchen about ten-thirty, but I'd already left for Syracuse."

This was a highly checkable alibi. And it sounded like the truth anyway. So good old Meg had lied to her.

Jerry gave her an alarmed look and got up cautiously. "She's okay, isn't she? Is there something infectious going around? As a matter of fact, are *you* okay?"

"Oh, she's fine," Quill ground her teeth. "I'm fine." Meg. The rat. "Yes, indeedy. We're both fine. For the moment."

"Well, good," Jerry said heartily. He began to back toward the door. "You're sure. About how fine you are, I mean."

"Oh, yes. I'm fine, too." She smiled. Jerry gave a visible start. Perhaps the smile wasn't as placatory as she'd meant it to be.

"Look, Quill. I can see you're upset about something." Quill stared at him for almost a minute. Here she was, beating up on innocent Jerry Grimsby who wanted to seduce her sister one week before her wedding to someone else, but clearly hadn't. "Not at all, Jerry. And I apologize for grabbing you and yelling at you. It's not your fault. I accept full responsibility. And when I get my hands on my sister, I'm going to . . . never mind." She could feel herself turn pink. If Meg was a rat, she, Quill, was a wart hog. Cappuccino dribbled all down the front of Jerry's tee-shirt. First Elmer Henry and now Jerry Grimsby. She was a double wart hog. "I am really sorry about grabbing your shirt, Jerry."

"Apology accepted." He eased himself out of the

office. “Although, I’ve been thinking. Maybe this *locum tenens* thing wasn’t such a hot idea.” By now, Jerry was in the foyer. He was walking backwards, rather rapidly, Quill thought.

“Maybe not,” she agreed. “I *am* sorry, Jerry. I think my sense of proportion’s slipped.”

“Not a bit of it.”

Jerry’s gait, she decided, could best be described as a scuttle.

“As a matter of fact this . . . ah . . . whatever, couldn’t have come at a more opportune time. There was a call from one of the waiters at Seasons on my answering machine last night. Tom said he thought some restaurant critic was in town. You know how they disguise themselves. Anyhow, whoever it was seems to have hated the food. At least, that was what the staff picked up from the conversation they overheard. The kitchen’s pretty concerned. And so am I. Maybe I should just go on back to Ithaca?”

“Oh,” Quill said, with what even she recognized as disproportionate relief, “must you?”

“Sure. I’ll just leave you and Meg alone.”

“I’m so sorry, Jerry. Believe me, there was just this . . . mix up. About where you really were last night. And you were so good to offer to help us out.”

“You don’t even need me,” Jerry said generously. “Bjarne can just about take charge in the kitchen. He’s a pretty good guy. You’ll be fine.”

Jerry had finally reached the oak door leading to the front drive. It was always kept open in summer. He backed all the way out into the drive. He waved. He turned to move out of sight, stopped, and stuck his head back into the foyer. "By the way. Bjarne agrees with me about the duck. I think you ought to speak to Meg about it. She's pretty reasonable underneath it all."

Quill wanted to shout something unprintable about her sister, but she didn't. She slammed the door shut, instead.

"Whoa," Dina said.

Quill turned around. Dina looked at her appraisingly. "Can I put the stapler back on the desk, now?"

"Yes, you can."

"And the phone?"

"Sure."

"You look a lot better. You don't look like you're going to throw the stapler or the phone at the nearest moving object. Not to mention start spraying the joint with a machine gun."

"I am not a violent person," Quill said. "I've never thrown anything at anybody in my whole entire life. And yes, I feel a lot better, now that Jerry Grimsby's going back to Ithaca."

"Then Bjarne's going to be in charge of the kitchen?"

"Of course. Why not? You heard Jerry. Bjarne even agrees about Duck Quilliam. He'll be fine."

"And Meg?"

"That little rat?" Quill considered her sister's behavior objectively. "I lied about feeling better. I'm madder than I was before."

Dina stuck the stapler back under the desk.

Quill decided to keep the oak door closed even though it was high summer and they never shut it until late evening. Then she decided to sit down until she calmed down. She sank onto the pale leather couch that sat in front of the cobblestone fireplace. The oriental rug, the leather couch, the oak floor and the tall vases filled with lilies had all been carefully selected to present the most appealing welcome to guests of the Inn. The most important part of the welcome was the attitude of the innkeeper, though, and she wasn't going to open the door until she got hold of herself.

"So," Dina said after a long moment of silence. "Are you going to, like, tell Meg that you scared Jerry Grimsby back to Ithaca?"

"I didn't scare Jerry into a thing," Quill said lamely. "Did I? He just sort of left. Didn't he? Yikes. I think I'm losing my mind. All I want to do is get her married. Was I completely and horribly awful?"

"Pretty much," Dina said comfortably.

Quill looked up to see Meg herself walking down the curved stairway to the foyer. She'd changed out of her nightshirt. She wore white cotton pants, a beige linen camp shirt and a very cute pair of Borg sandals with no socks. She even had a dash of lipstick on. It was pink, and it lightened her gray eyes. She was examining her cell phone with a frown.

"Hey," Quill said.

"Hey." Meg stuck the cell phone in the pocket of her camp shirt. "That was Jerry on the phone. And there's cinnamon focaccia all over the rug."

"I know," Quill said between her teeth. "So, Jerry called just now, did he?"

"He says there's an emergency at Seasons. Ha!" She laughed. "I'll just bet there's an emergency," she added scornfully. "Coward!"

"Oh?"

"He's on his way back to Ithaca," Meg scoffed. "He just couldn't handle a real gourmet kitchen. He's cut out on us, Quill. Beat feet. Left Bjarne in charge of the kitchen. Tell you what. You can't trust a chef that can't handle duck. Fact."

"I think Jerry's duck is pretty good," Dina said. "And I think Jerry himself is even better. As a matter of fact, he's close to heroic, in my book."

"Phuut!" Meg said. "I told him exactly what I think of him, too."

Dina frowned at Quill. Quill knew what the frown was all about. Jerry could have called Meg and told her that Quill had assaulted him (or was it battered him? Quill wasn't sure of the details of that particular felony,) right in the Inn foyer, and that he would never darken the Inn's door again, but he hadn't. He'd taken the blame for leaving them all in the lurch on himself. He'd been a complete and total gentleman. And now Meg was mad at him, probably for life, and it was very unjust. Quill felt awful.

She looked at her sister and stopped feeling awful. She started getting mad all over again. If Meg hadn't pulled what she'd pulled just now, poor Jerry would have remained unpersecuted, in charge of the kitchen

. . . and wildly attractive to Meg. She gripped her hair in both hands and pulled hard. It didn't help. "Meg. We need to talk."

Meg smiled sweetly at her. "About what?"

"You know very well what," Quill shouted furiously.

"Sorry, dear," Meg said. "No time. Andy and I are going to look at that house in Covert. As a matter of fact I hear him coming right now." She turned her head, and Quill did hear someone coming down the stairs. And it was Andy, who looked just as tired as he had when she'd seen him half an hour ago. Then his eyes lit on her sister and he looked tired but happy. "There you are. You're ready?"

"Yep." Meg tucked her arm into Andy's. "See ya, Sis."

Quill felt menacing. She didn't care. "You've got that right. And it's going to be sooner rather than later."

Andy bent forward and looked at Quill. "You look a little upset. Are you concerned about Maltby?"

"Who? Oh. Leo. Yes. I suppose . . . I mean, of course." Quill gathered her wits. She was a lousy innkeeper on top of everything else. Guests were a sacred trust, even if the guest in question was a rabble-rouser and a nudie-bar aficionado and a probable murderer. Well, Leo wasn't a sacred trust. But the Boom-Boom girls were guests, and they deserved better. "Is he okay?"

"If you can get him back to the hospital, it'd be a very good thing, Quill. He does have a concussion. And I'm afraid there's a possibility of a subdural hematoma. I tried to convince him that he should be under medical supervision, but I didn't get very far."

Quill set any thoughts of revenge on Meg aside. Temporarily. "Well that's not good at all, is it? What can we do?"

Andy reached into the pocket of his sports coat. "Here's a number for private nursing services. I left it with his wife—what's her name, Brenda something. I didn't really pay much attention to her." Andy's face was pink. Meg and Quill exchanged looks, warfare suspended. As a matter of fact, their former alliance was totally restored. Quill could tell with just one look. There wasn't a man under ninety-two who wouldn't pay attention to Brittney-Anne. "I don't think she really understood the urgency. Maybe you'll have more success with her than I."

"I doubt it," Quill said. "Didn't you notice how much trouble she has with polysyllables?"

"Huh?"

"Dumb," Meg added. "Dumber than dirt. I mean, she's pretty enough, I'll grant you that."

"Gosh, Meg. I wouldn't say that. I got a glimpse of her without all that makeup this morning. Yuck."

"Most of it from a tube, huh? You can do a lot with the right makeup."

"And what isn't from a tube is plastic," Quill agreed. "Or from Nadine Nickerson's Hemlock Hall of Beauty."

"Nadine's?" Andy said, puzzled.

"Wig," Meg said succinctly. "You thought all that

hair was hers? Oh, Andy." She gave his side an affectionate nudge. "Let's not be late for the realtor."

"I'm not the one standing around gossiping about Brenda," Andy said.

"Brittney, Brenda, whatever." Quill drew Andy to the front door. "You guys have a good time. Everything's under control here."

Meg dug her heels into the carpet. "Wait. Jerry's gone. What about the kitchen?"

"I'll talk to Bjarne right now," Quill promised.

"You'll have to call him," Meg said. "He's supposed to be off today." She glanced at her watch. "Breakfast is over, but we're booked solid for lunch. It's the Hadassah. They've been here lots of times, and they know what to expect. As a matter of fact, they're planning on making the once-a-month lunch in summer a regular thing for the foreseeable future."

"That's terrific!"

"Just be sure and get him in here, okay?"

"I'll do that."

Quill finally got them both out the door. She waited until Andy's dark blue Mercedes had disappeared down the length of the driveway. Then she lay down on the couch and stared up at the foyer ceiling. Parts of the Inn dated back to the seventeenth century when it was a way station on the trapper's trail up to Canada. The foyer was one of these. The beams that crossed the ceiling were three-hundred-year-old oak. Quill crossed her hands on her stomach and contemplated the knots in the wood. They made a very pleasing pattern. She was just going to collect herself. Just for a moment.

". . . wake her up!" an indignant voice said in her ear.

Quill woke up. "Dina?"

"Sorry, Quill. Hangovers take me like that, too. I told him to leave you alone. You needed a little rest."

The beamed ceiling swam into view. She squinted at it. The whorls in the middle beam looked like the face of a very old man. She turned her head. Dina's face was upside down. She was standing at the head of the couch looking down at her. Quill sat up and swung her feet to the floor.

"Bit too much to drink last night?" The other voice was male, diffident, and sympathetic.

"I am *not* hungover," Quill said. "I'm sleep-deprived."

"Gibsons," Dina said wisely.

Standing next to Dina was a vaguely familiar figure. "Agent Purvis!" Quill snapped totally awake.

"Shh!" Dina said.

Quill patted futilely at her hair, which was all over her face. "My goodness, what are you doing here?"

The last (and only) time she'd met FBI agent Melvin Purvis his visit had been followed by a particularly unpleasant murder. Quill got to her feet and shook his hand. Agent Purvis (no relation to the first agent Purvis, who'd spearheaded the capture of the notorious John Dillenger) was in his thirties, round-faced, with long-lashed hazel eyes. "You've met Dina Muir, our receptionist?"

"Yes ma'am." He smiled at Dina. He had a particularly sweet smile. "Copepods, right?"

"Right," Dina said. "Although I have to say I've been pretty disillusioned about copepods, lately."

"Now that's a shame." Agent Purvis shook his head. "Has something more interesting come along?"

Dina drew breath. Quill didn't want to hear it. She was afraid it would have to do with fake eyelashes and silicone implants and the generally more glamorous life of ecdysiasts. "Is there something we can do for you?" Quill drew him toward her office, where they would be out of the way of any curious guest. Hazel eyes and curling lashes notwithstanding, Agent Purvis always looked exactly like an FBI agent. In addition to the regulation narrow tie, white shirt and short haircut, his shoulder holster was usually visible under his sports coat.

Except he wasn't wearing any of those things at the moment.

Quill stopped and blinked at him. He was dressed in a polo shirt with a Ralph Lauren logo on it and white cargo shorts. His hair was longer. And he carried a hunter green Eddie Bauer duffle bag. Quill rubbed her face. She must still be half-asleep. "You're undercover, Agent Purvis!"

"Pardon, ma'am?"

"I'll get you guys some coffee," Dina offered.

"That's a really good idea," Quill said gratefully.

Dina headed through the archway to the kitchen. Quill shut the door to her office and sat down behind her desk. Agent Purvis took a chair from her small conference table and sat down across from her.

"Actually," she said. "I've been expecting you."

He frowned.

"I mean, not because anyone's mentioned you. It's, you know." She glanced up at the ceiling, where poor Leo Maltby lay two floors up. Agent Purvis looked up at the ceiling, too.

"I'm not sure what you're talking about," he said.

"Oh. Of course. Sorry," Quill said wisely.

"I'm here to check in."

"You are?"

"Yes, I have a reservation."

"You do? My goodness. I didn't . . . excuse me." Quill turned to her desktop and keyed in a request for the reservations list. "I don't . . . Oh!" Of course! He was undercover.

"I think I can trust Miss Muir to keep it quiet, Quill. The thing is, can I trust you?"

"Of course. Does Myles . . . well, he would, wouldn't he. I wondered why he hadn't said anything to me. Not that he would," she added hastily. "I mean he doesn't talk about that sort of thing in any inappropriate way."

"The decision was made yesterday," Agent Purvis said. "And the arrangements were made this morning. Now if I could just get the key?"

"Certainly." She smiled at Dina, who came through the door with a tray of coffee in her hands. "Could you just get Agent Pur—"

"Shh!" Dina said.

Quill glanced at the computer screen. "I mean, Mr. Kelvin, the key to . . ."

"220," Dina said briskly. "Here it is, Mr. Kelvin. We hope you enjoy your stay at the Inn at Hemlock Falls."

"Thank you." He slipped the key into his pocket, grabbed his duffle bag and was out the door before Quill had a chance to offer him coffee.

"Well," Quill said. "Now *this* is interesting."

"It is, isn't it?" Dina sat in the chair Agent Purvis had vacated and poured herself a cup of coffee. Then she poured one for Quill. "Do you suppose he's here about Leo Maltby?"

"Who else?"

They both looked up at the ceiling. Quill gave a start. "Gosh! I completely forgot about the nurse. Do you suppose I should go up and try to talk him into it?"

"Why don't you call him on the house phone and talk him into it?" Dina said. "It's easier." She waved the dreaded fistful of While-You-Were-Outs at her. "And a couple of these phone calls sounded important . . ." She broke off. "What are you doing?"

"Banging my head against the desk."

"Does it help?"

"Yes." Quill sat up. "It was quite refreshing, actually. Okay, this is me. Getting control over the day." She glanced at the desk clock. "Except it's after eleven-thirty. Why did you let me sleep so long? Rats. First thing—get a nurse for Mr. Maltby, so the poor guy doesn't drop dead playing poker." She tapped in the extension for 321. "It's busy."

"You know what? I'll go." Dina drained her coffee cup. "It's like John's always saying, Quill, "you have to delegate more. I can handle this."

"Great." Dina was right. John Raintree had been their business manager for years before he went into his own consulting business, and Quill missed the dailiness of their talks more than she could say. "You know what? You can handle a lot of responsibility, Dina. You really can. I'm giving you an instant promotion. Assistant manager. What do you think?"

Dina shoved her glasses up her nose with her forefinger. "Really?"

"Really."

"So, like, is there a raise with this promotion?"

"Absolutely."

"How much?"

"I don't know yet."

"I'm cool with that. It wouldn't be as much as Doreen's promotion, but that's okay."

"As much as Doreen's promotion."

"Well, yeah. I mean, like she's event co-coordinator, tour director, she's got like a ton more to do now."

"I guess it wouldn't be as much as Doreen's promotion, but more than you're making now. How's that?"

"And would the assistant manager, like, take over whenever you're not around?"

Quill, thumbing through the list of telephone calls to be returned, instantly saw a lot of advantages to Dina's taking over when she wasn't around. For one thing, Dina could return this call from Carol Ann Spinoza.

Carol Ann's sneaky, spiteful behavior rolled right off Dina's back. Carole Ann was stupid as well as mean, and she was impressed by titles. Maybe she should make Dina vice-president in charge of management. And the call from Miriam Doncaster—Dina could return that, too. Miriam regarded Dina in a very maternal light, and she would never accuse her of betraying her gender. And finally, it might help solve Dina's perennial financial problems as an improvident graduate student. "That's exactly what this assistant manager would do. Take over when the manager's not around. Here. Take care of these phone calls, will you?"

Dina took the pile of While-You-Were-Outs with a pleased air.

"Now, whenever I'm out of the Inn, Dina, I'll have my cell phone with me. So if there's any kind of problem, you give me a call. Okay?"

"So I'm the new assistant manager?"

"Congratulations."

The phone rang. Dina picked it up. "Welcome to the Inn at Hemlock Falls," she said. "This is the assistant manager. Huh? Oh. Sure." She held the phone out. "It's Ms. Schmidt."

"Where you been?" Marge demanded. "Didja get my message?"

Quill made a face. Dina held up the third message slip: Emergency Chamber meeting 11:30. Resort.

"I'm on my way." Quill thanked Marge for reminding her about the meeting. She could tell there wasn't a lot of conviction in her voice. Then she hung up.

"The Emergency Chamber meeting?"

"Yes. Ah, Dina, why don't you . . ."

"No."

"Committee meetings are a large part of one's managerial duties."

"No. Besides, I'm a lousy note-taker."

"You can't be a lousy note-taker. You've had six million years of graduate school."

Dina sighed. "More like seven million. And really, Quill, they'd be as ticked off if you weren't on the board as they are that you're on it?"

Quill took a minute to sort this out. "They're ticked off? At me?"

"Well, hel-lo. Who was it that supported Lovejoy's Nudie Bar and Grill on national TV?"

"They can't be *that* ticked off," Quill said.

CHAPTER 10

They were that ticked off. The Chamber was so ticked off that for once, everyone had listened to Carol Ann Spinoza, and by the time Quill got there, they'd voted to hold all future Chamber of Commerce meetings in the conference room at the new Resort, and Quill had to pretend her feelings weren't well and truly hurt (which they were) and that the loss of the monthly lunch business didn't hurt, either (which it did).

She also had to pretend she wasn't nervous about the splendor of the conference facilities provided by the Resort at Hemlock Falls. All the Inn needed at the moment was some significant competition.

The conference room was comfortably large. The conference table was round; much better for meetings. Members didn't have to crane their necks if someone else on the same side of the table was speaking up. And at one end of the room was a kitchenette, so that lunch could be served right there at the table. And everything had a pleasant smell of fresh paint and new carpet.

"Pretty nice," Harland Peterson said. Quill was sitting between Harland and Ferris Rodman because when she'd walked into the meeting fifteen minutes late, Miriam Doncaster hastily filled the empty seat between her and Marge Schmidt with her tote bag.

"Yes, it is," Quill said uneasily.

"We aim to please," Rodman said. He smiled at Quill, the way Bruce the shark smiled at Robert Shaw in the last minutes of *Jaws.* "And how is Mr. Maltby this morning?"

"Not well," Quill said.

"Heard he checked himself out of the hospital."

"Yes," Quill said worriedly, "Andy thinks he ought to have a nurse."

Rodman looked bored.

Harland shifted his large frame in the padded conference chair. "Pretty comfortable here, too, Rodman. Nice job."

Rodman nodded. "Good to know you approve."

Adela Henry whacked the table with the mayor's gavel. She was dressed in royal purple, from head to toe. Quill herself might have forgone the orange blouse under the pantsuit, but there was no denying the overall effect. "Might we have some silence, please?" She frowned majestically at Quill. "You missed this, because you were late, Quill, but I began this meeting by thanking our newest member for the loan of these splendid facilities. Much nicer than the cramped space formerly available to us. Thank you again, Ferris."

Loan? There wasn't any charge for the space? Ferris Rodman, a new Chamber member? Quill nodded at him. He raised his hand in a brief salute.

"We had to dispense with the reading of the minutes since you weren't here," Adela continued. "But since this is an *ex facto* meeting . . ."

"*Ex parte,* Adela," Howie Murchinson said. He winked at Quill.

"Whatever. Anyway, it isn't necessary. We do have two urgent items of new business . . ."

Quill nudged Harland and whispered, "Where's Elmer?"

Adela whacked the gavel. "Silence, please! We have a great deal to do today. Sidebar conversations will not be tolerated under *this* administration."

"This administration?" Quill looked at Harland. Harland shrugged.

"The mayor," Adela said, "is at home taking a well-deserved break from his duties as president of this body. If you had been here on time, Quill, I would not have to repeat myself. And I might add that I have asked the town librarian to take over your duties as secretary since you appear to take them quite cavalierly."

Miriam sent her a smug look. Quill had tried for years to get Miriam to take over her duties as secretary. And there she was, taking notes. And looking smug.

Quill shrank down in her chair. Then, because she'd never before sat in a Chamber meeting where she hadn't been taking notes herself, she pulled out her notebook and a charcoal pencil.

"First order of business is a short address by Mr. Ferris Rodman. He will keep us *au fait* . . ."

"*Au courant,* Adela," Howie said. "Good grief."

"Whatever. Mr. Rodman will let us know the status of the Resort Gala plans. And may I take this opportunity to once again welcome you to full Chamber of Commerce status."

"Thank you." Ferris Rodman had abandoned his usual white shirt and windbreaker for a white shirt and sports coat. His pocket protector was blue plastic with white letters that proclaimed ROCOR Construction. Harvey Bozzel clearly had not been successful in selling Rodman any fancy promotional items.

"I'm a plain-spoken man," Ferris Rodman said. "And I like to keep things simple. Thank you for the opportunity to become a member of this fine organization." He bowed slightly in Adela's direction. Adela bridled with pleasure. "The plans for the Gala opening are coming along well. The Governor will be able to attend . . ." He paused for applause. He got it. ". . . and we have promises from Channel 10 and Channel 13 in Rochester that they will be there with bells on and cameras rolling."

More applause.
"The theme for the evening is Las Vegas night."
Quill sat up.
"All Chamber members are invited, of course. And it will be black tie. So ladies, I hope you will patronize Ms. West's dress shop for formal gowns. I believe she will be getting a special shipment in, just for this occasion." Rodman nodded to Esther, who smiled happily at everyone in general. "There will be champagne, a little sophisticated gambling, and of course . . ."
Quill's eyes met Marge Schmidt's. Neither one of them had liked Ferris Rodman when he'd swept into Hemlock Falls several years ago—Marge, because he was a challenge to her supremacy as the richest person in Tompkins County, and Quill, because she had her suspicions that Rodman had more than just one evening's gambling on his mind. Marge nodded told ya! and her hand shot up.
"Just a moment, Marge. And of course you'll all want to meet Mr. Schwarzenegger."
"*Arnold* Schwarzenegger?" Miriam shrieked. "Oh, my god!"
"Is that the guy who did them *Terminator* movies?" Harland asked Quill.
"And the guy who's the governor of California," Quill said. "Good grief."
Harland scraped one work-roughened hand over his jaw. "Have to say that's my kind of guy."
Rodman raised both hands, in a not-very-rigorous attempt to quell the excitement. "I can't promise that

Arnie's going to be able to make it, but I have his assurances that he'll do his best. Right now, he's scheduled to tour the Finger Lakes wineries as part of a joint venture between the growers here and the Napa valley . . ."

"That's in California, people," Esther said excitedly.

". . . and I've put in a request that he stop by the Resort on our opening night." Rodman's sharp blue eyes rested on Marge. "There's a number of notable spots in Hemlock Falls Mr. Schwarzenegger might like to see. We have, if I do say so myself, the best diner food in North America. And I can't think of a better introduction to Hemlock Falls than Betty Hall's famous Garbage Plate."

Marge's hand went down. She looked pleased. Furious at this defection, Quill shot her own hand in the air.

Rodman ignored it. "Thank you." He sat down to loud handclapping and a few cheers. Adela got to her feet, her considerable bosom heaving with emotion. "All this," she said. "And Mr. Schwarzenegger, too! Mr. Rodman, we are overwhelmed. Overwhelmed. Especially since it was one of our very own who had a hand in that debacle we imposed upon you yesterday." Her glance swept patronizingly over Quill.

Quill half-rose from her seat, waving her hand like a cheerleader on the losing side. Adela's gaze swept over her as if she didn't exist. "Which brings us to yesterday's press conference. Second order of business is containment," Adela said briskly. "After the debacle on national television yesterday . . ."

"Regional," Quill said.

"I beg your pardon?"

"Channel 15 is regional, not national."

"The chair has not recognized you, Quill."

Quill shrank back down into her own chair. Then she sketched a tiny little Elmer sitting outside a doghouse with a sorrowful look on his face.

". . . after the shame of Hemlock Falls had been broadcast all the way to San Francisco . . ."

Quill drew a tiny little Quill and another, smaller dog house.

". . . I requested aid from our very own public relations expert, Harvey Bozzel. Harvey? You have five minutes." When Adela nodded, as she did now, all of her double chins folded into her neck. Quill debated a moment, then drew a large Adela with huge double chins. She added a tiny little mustache, SS insignia, and a Nazi salute.

Harvey, president of Hemlock Falls' best (and only) advertising agency, bounced to his feet. He smoothed his carefully gelled blonde hair and assumed a sober expression. "I have already issued press releases to the major media. The voice of the people must be heard. It is time for dissent. It is time for a referendum!"

This was met with a puzzled silence.

"Actually," Howie Murchison said after a reflective moment, "that's a very good idea. A referendum could reverse the decision of the zoning board."

"And what's that referendum thing when it's at home?" Harland asked.

"We get a majority of the townspeople to vote against the commercial licensing of MacAvoy's property. That'd be the easiest way. The sale of the property was probably contingent on the licensing, so it'd mean Bernie would have to give Maltby his money back." Howie rubbed his jaw. "On the other hand, we've got a surplus in the town's accounts. Maybe the town could agree to buy the property from Bernie. At any rate, the referendum's a good way to start." He looked at Harvey with surprised approval. "Good idea, Harvey. Very good idea."

An odd look passed over Ferris Rodman's face. Quill, intrigued, made a quick sketch of his expression, concealing the sketch with her left hand.

Harvey's chest puffed out an inch or so. "The nation must know that we will not tolerate nudie bars in Hemlock Falls."

Adela gaveled with enthusiasm. "Hear, hear."

"There is no more effective voice than the voice of the people," Harvey continued. "And in that light, I have written a song."

"A song?" Miriam said.

"A protest song." Harvey reached beneath the table and set out a boom box. "I've scheduled a march to get out the vote. The march is scheduled for three o'clock this afternoon. We will begin on Main Street and proceed via this route." He reached beneath the table again. He emerged with a stack of bright pink paper. He took a sheet, divided the pile in half then passed one half to Adela and the other to Ferris Rodman. They each took one and passed the piles on.

"You'll note that the proposal for the referendum is on one side. The lyrics and the map are on the other. The song," he added importantly, "is set to 'The Battle Hymn of the Republic.' "

"Which is available to all the public," Adela interjected.

"Do you mean that it's in the public domain?" Howie asked.

"Whatever."

Harvey cleared his throat. "I recorded this last night, with Adela's help. That's Mrs. Dookie Shuttleworth on the organ. We'll run through it once on tape, then we'll all sing it together." He stabbed the boom box and the introductory strains of "The Battle Hymn of the Republic" flooded the room just as Quill's cell phone vibrated urgently in her skirt pocket.

She pulled the phone out, stuck one finger in her ear, and stabbed at the buttons with her thumb. It seemed to be Dina, but with the uncertain notes of the organ bouncing around the room, Quill couldn't be sure. She excused herself to Harland (who was beating the table in time to the music) and went out the door that led to the parking lot, the phone still held to her ear. "Dang!" she clicked the phone off and punched the button for missed calls.

"Handy things," Marge observed behind her, "but they take a bit of getting used to."

Quill pushed the end button. She hoped whatever Dina wanted could wait. "I'm glad you came out after me. It's about Rodman, isn't it?"

Marge squinted up at the sky, which was hot and very blue. "I got my suspicions about that good ol' boy, that's for sure. Let's get out of this sun. I'm gettin' a headache."

"There's a flu-y sort of thing going around," Quill sympathized. Maybe that's what was making Meg crazier than normal. Maybe it was making herself crazier than normal, too.

"I don't get the flu. Here. Might as well sit in that gazebo."

Quill followed her to the first of the four gazebos that lined the newly sanded beach of the Hemlock River. "This really is nice," Quill said regretfully as they settled across from one another. The river water ran a clear green almost at their feet. The banks were lined with neat plates of the rough shale that formed most of the land in this part of New York. "The Resort ought to do pretty well, don't you think?"

"If you mean do I think that it'll cut into some of your business up there at the Inn, I won't lie to you. Prob'ly will."

"I thought once Rodman abandoned the idea for the boutique hotel at the old Civil War Cemetery we didn't have anything to worry about."

Marge snorted. "Wouldn't be too sure that he abandoned it. Just couldn't get the thing up this year, what with it being a crime scene and all."

This reference to that previous case made it easy for Quill to voice the question that was on both their minds. "So do you think he's trying to go ahead with it? Turn this into a gambling casino after all?"

Marge swatted the air, as if chasing a wasp. "We aren't supposed to know a thing about that."

Quill thought back to the nighttime foray they'd made into Rodman's office some months before. "But we do."

Marge expelled a long breath. "Yeah. We do."

"Did you see how he just sort of rolled over any possible opposition?" Quill was so exasperated she couldn't sit still. She jumped up and walked to the railing. "Esther and the evening gowns. The Governor. Arnold Schwarzenegger! My hat. Does he think we're idiots?" She looked over the railing in disgust. "And his taste is strictly second-rate hotel. Look at this! Geraniums! How boring."

"He's slick," Marge admitted. "But the hotel's pretty nice."

"He even had you going for a minute," Quill said. "I mean, is Arnold Schwarzenegger about to eat Betty's Garbage Plate? I ask you!" She turned and got the full benefit of Marge's basilisk stare. "It's famous even without Arnold Schwarzenegger eating it," she added hastily. "I love it, myself."

"Right." Marge said dryly. "Las Vegas night, huh? Looks to me like the thin edge of the wedge. I know how these types think, Quill. Let the dumb natives get a little taste of the action in a Las Vegas night. Then just slip in a little amendment to the town code to let gambling in on Saturday nights. Then . . ." she swept the air again. "Hello, Vegas."

"I don't want Hemlock Falls to turn into Las Vegas." Quill admitted. "I mean, Las Vegas is just fine. But you can go there and come home again. You don't have all that neon in your backyard. Oh, nuts, Marge. Look at me." She sat back down on the bench. "Am I really turning into a bigot?"

"Why're you a bigot if you got an opinion?"

"I don't know," Quill grumbled. "I'm against gambling. I'm against what Leo Maltby stands for. But it's wrong to want to step on somebody else's right to choose. I don't want anybody to step on *my* right to choose. I'm turning into one of those smarmily smug conservatives who think they know everything. I don't want to think of myself like that. Hey, I would have marched at Berkeley if I hadn't been two years old."

"Well I don't want gambling in Hemlock Falls 'cause it'll knock the heck out of the value of my real estate and my insurance premiums'll go sky high. I don't give a horse's patoot for the rest of it. But it seems to me that folks have got a right to their opinions, same as we do, and that what decides it is a vote. But it's gotta be a vote based on the facts. Not a vote that's been manipulated by Mr. Thinks-he's-got-a-leg-over Rodman."

"Right," Quill said.

"So, what are the facts?" Marge asked rhetorically. "The facts are that we got two threats to life in Hemlock Falls as we know it: Rodman and his gambling and Maltby."

"Right."

"So somehow, we gotta get these guys out of town."

"No, we don't," Quill said patiently. "We have to let the town know all the facts so that the votes will be fair. I mean, Harvey's referendum idea was a stroke of genius!"

Marge's look was combined equally of pity and contempt. "Votin's private, last time I looked at the Constitution."

Quill, while taken with the idea that Marge spent any time at all reading the Constitution, got to the point. "What do you mean?"

"You got a look at that Brittney-Anne? You think the men of this town are gonna vote to put her on the first train out of here?"

"I am very glad that we don't share the same view of human nature," Quill said stiffly. "I have perfect confidence in the democratic process."

The noise from the conference room, which had remained in the background for some time, now escalated as the doors to the parking lot opened. The Chamber meeting was over. Adela and Harvey led a procession of members outside. Harvey's boom box was playing the orchestral refrain of "The Battle Hymn of the Republic" at full volume. Instead of the "Glory, Glory. Hallelujah!" part, though, the crowd was singing: "keep the town from naked wi-i-immin, keep our folks from wretched si-i-in-in," and Quill stuck her fingers in her ears, more from annoyance over the discordance than from the lyrics. Marge grinned at her and mouthed. "Get my point?" which made Quill so cross that she snapped, "Fine. You're right. I give up. What do *you* think we should do?"

Marge waited until the last of the cars had exited the parking lot. "Poor old Maltby's got to go."

"He's pretty determined. And it's weird, Marge. You think he'd behave more like Rodman, try to keep a low profile and slip in sideways, if you know what I mean. But he absolutely shouts for attention. It's as if he wants all this furor."

"Guy didn't strike me as the brightest bulb in the chandelier."

"Well, there is that," Quill admitted. "But still."

"Thing is, he's the likeliest suspect in the MacAvoy murder, isn't he?"

"It wasn't MacAvoy," Quill pointed out. "It was a smalltime hood named Caprese."

"No kiddin'?"

"No kidding. And *she,*" Quill waited for an amazed response from Marge, but didn't get one, "Antonia Caprese, that is, is supposedly connected. You know. Like Tony Soprano connected."

"You don't say."

"And there's more, Marge. You remember this last March?"

"Of course I remember last March. It's how come we know that Rodman's applied for a casino license."

"You remember the FBI agent. Melvin Purvis? No relation," she added quickly.

"Yeah."

"He's back."

"Back?"

"Checked in this morning. But he's undercover. You can't tell anyone. I'm breaking a federal confidence to tell you that much."

"A federal what?"

"Anyhow, you know what that means."

"I never heard of a federal confidence."

"I mean that the FBI is involved. They deal with interstate crime, not just local murders." Quill leaned forward. "Whatever Maltby's involved with is bigger than Hemlock Falls."

Marge looked as if she were about to say "big deal," but she didn't. "So we got a mobbed-up guy parked in one of your fancy suites? You think we should wait for the FBI to haul him away? That'll take months. Years. These guys don't move all that fast. Look here, Quill. You said yourself the FBI doesn't give a hoot for a little local murder. And I'll bet ya they're not after a small-fry like Maltby. Oh, no. If this Purvis is back in Hemlock Falls, he's not after Maltby. He's after Rodman."

"Wow," Quill said. "I'll bet you're right. I mean, when he was first here, he was after Rodman, wasn't he?"

"I thought he was here because of the threats against that judge."

"Justice," Quill corrected automatically. "Chief Justice. That's what he said. But it may not have been what he meant."

Both of them shook their heads over the lack of candor in federally funded law-enforcement agencies.

"So if Maltby's gonna go, we gotta take care of it.

You think he offed this Antonia Caprese?"

"I don't know," Quill admitted. "I thought so at first. But then he was attacked in the parking lot. But the attack . . ." Quill bit her lip. "Marge. I hate even thinking this. But we've got to consider it. Do you suppose someone from Hemlock Falls beat Leo up?"

"Tried to run him out of town?" Marge didn't seem to feel as miserably depressed at this prospect as Quill did. "Maybe. Can't think of who it might be, though. The kind of bozo who'd pull that is the kind of bozo who'd spend half his time in a strip joint anyways."

Quill sighed. It had to be said. Successful detectives couldn't afford sentiment, and friendship must always be set aside in the pursuit of justice. "What if it were a woman? The Women Against Crimes Against Women committee is pretty upset."

"T'uh! Who? Miriam? Forget it. Esther? Adela? Hardly. Those guys are all mouth and no action."

"There's . . . you know, Carol Ann."

Marge grinned. "Well, well, well. She's mean enough. She's dumb enough. And you know what? A convicted felon can't hold the position of tax assessor."

"Well!" Quill said. "Wouldn't that be a shame."

"Sure make me cry in my beer."

They smiled companionably at each other.

Quill looked at her watch. It was past one o'clock, long past time for her to get back to the Inn. "So if Leo's mugging has nothing to do with the body in the MacAvoy barn, there's a very strong possibility that he did dispose of poor Antonia Caprese. We need to get more information about that mugging, Marge."

"So you and me are gonna talk to Leo? Or that chippie wife of his?"

Quill shook her head. "We need to talk to the one person who seems to care about him, even though she is his ex-wife. Sheree Maltby. And I'm going back to the Inn to find her right now."

CHAPTER 11

Quill walked into a suspiciously quiet Inn. There were no waiters tidying up the remnants of the lunch hour. No murmur of activity from the kitchen, no sounds of happy, chattering guests floating in from the outside lawns.

Dina sat slumped behind the reception desk. She looked up as Quill came in the open front door and said, "I quit."

"You quit?"

"This assistant manager job sucks."

"Oh, dear," Quill said. She looked around a little helplessly. "Um. Where is everybody?"

"Where have you *been?*" Dina said. "You said you were going to keep your cell phone on!"

Quill patted her skirt pocket and took her cell phone out. "I did keep it on. I . . . oops. Dang. I guess I punched the off button instead of the end button. They should make these things larger."

The Inn wasn't completely deserted. Distant thumps and scrapes echoed down the stairwell. Quill turned her cell phone on and put it back in her pockct. "What's that?"

"The police," Dina said.

"The police? Oh, no!" Quill started up the stairs.

"Stop," Dina said. "He'll just make you come back down again."

"Who will? Not Davy."

"It's not Davy. It's Agent Purvis. He ordered everybody out."

"Agent Purvis ordered everybody out? Of my Inn! Why?"

"So he won't let you up there. Davy is up there, too, but he doesn't mind at all when you go to the scene of the crime. He likes it. He says half the time you . . ."

"What crime?!"

"It's Mr. Maltby."

Quill sank down on the couch. "Mr. Maltby? Oh, no. Did he die? This is terrible. He wasn't . . . murdered?"

Dina nodded miserably. "Yep. And it's my fault, Quill. Totally." She burst into tears. Quill almost burst into tears, too. She always did when somebody else started to cry. Instead, she rose to her feet and shepherded Dina into her office. She settled her tear-stained receptionist next to her on the couch, got out the Kleenex, and patted her back until the sobs subsided to hiccups. "Okay. Are you feeling able to talk about it?"

"It was the nurse," Dina said tragically. "At least, they think it was the nurse. I went up to 321 to talk Mr. Maltby into hiring one, and he said fine, sure, whatever, he was tired of being nagged at. I called that number

Andy left and she was here right away. I mean, like," Dina snapped her fingers, "twenty minutes. Tops. After she got here, Sheree and Norrie Ferguson came downstairs and said the nurse had thrown them out. Sheree was laughing about it. Said the nurse made Leo dump out his beer. She even got him to trash away his cigar. And she told Sheree to take a walk, that Leo needed total darkness to help recover from his concussion and that," Dina added in an awed voice, "was exactly what he got."

"How did he die?"

Dina shook her head, tears spilling onto her cheeks. Quill patted her back and handed her another Kleenex. "Smothered."

"Ugh."

"With a pillow."

"Oh, dear."

"One of the new goose-down ones. Doreen said we'll have to throw it out, if we ever get it back, that is. And they're expensive, Quill."

"That's all right." Quill guided her gently back to the problem at hand. "Who discovered the body?"

"Poor Kathleen. She was checking up on the housekeeping staff. Doreen told her she had to make random spot checks to make sure nobody was skimping on the job. She went into 321 about a half an hour ago. She called out 'housekeeping,' just like you're supposed to and of course, nobody answered because poor Leo was already—" Dina stopped mid-sentence, took a deep breath, and pinched her knee. "It's okay. I'm okay.

Anyway, of course she went in when no one answered. And there he was. Dead as a doornail. And the nurse was gone. Disappeared." Dina tried to snap her fingers again, but they were too soggy. She swallowed hard. "And I made the call. I got her here."

"You had absolutely no idea what would happen," Quill said fiercely. "None, do you hear me? This was a setup, pure and simple."

"I thought about that." Dina scrubbed her eyes with the balled-up Kleenex. "But it can't be Andy's fault. That doesn't make sense."

"Andy's fault? Oh! Because he gave you the number. No, it doesn't make sense. But it will, Dina. I promise you. We'll figure this out."

Dina nodded. "I'm glad you're on the case," she said simply. "I need to wash my face."

"Okay. Use my bathroom."

Dina disappeared into the small half-bath attached to the office. Over the splash of water, Quill called, "So what happened after Kathleen found the body?"

Dina reappeared, clutching a hand towel. "Well, she screamed, of course. But nobody heard her at first."

Quill had heard the thumps of the police from the third floor just now as she stood in the foyer. If Kathleen had been screaming, someone downstairs should have noticed. "You didn't hear her?"

"Nope."

"Why not?"

"Because the Hadassah were stomping all over the place and raising holy heck."

"They were?"

Dina looked stricken. "I told you I quit, didn't I? I'm just not any good at this assistant manager stuff, Quill. There's a lot more to it than meets the eye."

Quill waited.

"Nobody called Bjarne to come in early and take over when you . . . I mean when Jerry went back to Ithaca."

Quill covered her eyes with her hands. "That's my fault."

"Well, yeah, it was. But the assistant manager should be able to handle stuff like that. So the Hadassah show up and, like, they were supposed to have this special meal?"

Quill shook her head. "Meg takes care of that. And we haven't exactly been talking latcly."

"Um. Thing is, she's all hipped on this duck recipe."

"And?"

"And she'd ordered a pile of duck breasts to make duck Quilliam for the Hadassah. Only Jerry told the *sous* chefs this morning that Meg's duck recipe wasn't fit to feed gilts, much less humans . . ."

"Wait a minute, guilts?"

"G-I-L-T-S," Dina spelled out carefully. "It's a baby pig."

"Oh."

"Baby pigs are, like, not discriminating in what they eat. See, when Jerry said Duck Quilliam wasn't fit to feed gilts . . ."

"Got it," Quill said. "So Jerry left without telling them what to do with the duck."

"Right. And Bjarne wasn't supposed to be here until two o'clock, his regular time. So Kunte, you know Kunte . . ."

"Of course I do!" Quill snapped. "He's unusually good. Meg's been thinking of promoting . . . Quill smacked herself on the head. "Now I'm doing it."

"Doing what?"

"Dina! What happened with the duck?"

"Jerry said under no circumstances to serve Meg's duck recipe. He was going to make *his* duck recipe. But he was gone, and Bjarne was the only other person in the kitchen who knew how to make it. But we did have a lot of pork. And Kunte's pork recipe is just the nuts. And Bjarne wasn't due in until two. Meg was going to put it on the menu, anyway, the pork, I mean."

"We served pork to the Hadassah?"

"Yep."

Quill didn't say anything.

"Kunte's from Africa! He didn't know!"

"So the Hadassah left."

"Well, not right away. They hollered and screamed a bit. Which is why I didn't hear Kathleen right away. So Kathleen came running downstairs hollering there was a dead man in 321. *Then* they left. Pretty fast, as a matter of fact."

"Hm," Quill said. "So. Where is everybody?"

"If you mean everybody on our side, they're all in the kitchen. If you mean Agent Purvis, I mean Mr. Kelvin, he and Davy are up on the third floor. If you mean the guests, well, the only ones left are Sheree and the

Boom-Boom girls. I think they're in the Tavern Lounge getting looped. Everybody else left."

"A lot of people checked out?"

"A lot of people *ran* out. I'm going to have to go through and put all the bills on the credit card numbers they gave me when they checked in."

"That might be a nice quiet thing to do right now." Quill gave her another Kleenex. "You've had quite a day."

"You don't mind that I quit?"

"As long as you didn't quit the receptionist job."

"No, I didn't quit that. I would if I could afford it. I have just screwed everything up. And I'm an accessory to murder!"

"To be an accessory to murder you have to mean it." Quill sighed. "You did the best you could, Dina. What a nightmare."

"It was a nightmare," Dina agreed. "But I feel better, now. You're a good sympathizer, Quill."

"You had an absolutely awful time of it."

"I did," Dina said tragically.

"Are you going to be okay, now?"

"I think so. Where are you going?"

"A number of things need to be seen to. But I'll be right here at the Inn. And my cell phone's on. Call me if you need me, okay? You've handled this very well, sweetie. Very well. I wouldn't have done a thing differently. Well, I might have stopped Kunte from serving pork to the Hadassah, and I would have made sure that Bjarne came in at eleven instead of two, but you did everything else perfectly."

"Thanks." She looked up as Quill went out the doors. "In case I decide that I want to be assistant manager again—what is it that you're going to do first?"

Quill blinked at Dina's resilience. "Staff first, then the police. I'll be in the kitchen for a bit."

She crossed through the dining room, noting with dismay that the tables hadn't been cleared. Half-filled glasses of wine, cloudy water glasses, baskets of half-eaten bread, and stained napkins spread across the room like the detritus of a retreating army. She pushed open the swinging doors to the kitchen and walked in.

Bjarne looked up at her entrance, a carafe of brandy in one hand. The other hand was on Kathleen Kiddermeister's shoulder. Kathleen was seated at the birch prep table. A large, empty tumbler sat in front of her filled with the dregs of what looked like more brandy.

"I quit," Kathleen said.

"I quit, too," Bjarne said.

Behind Kathleen, two *sous* chefs and her wine steward were crowded against the bank of dishwashers: Elizabeth Chou, Peter Hairston, and Kunte Mgwambe. Dirty dishes were everywhere. The kitchen was one of Quill's favorite places at the Inn. The flagstone floor, the copper pans hanging from the stone walls, the cobblestone fireplace with the grate now filled with summer daisies were usually a refuge. Now it looked like a war zone.

Quill didn't say anything for a moment.

"Miss Quill?" Kunte Mgwambe asked tentatively. "I

am so, so sorry." His large brown eyes filled with tears.
"I chased the ladies away!" Elizabeth burst into tears. Peter turned bright pink. Kathleen raised a glass of brandy to her lips and hiccupped. Bjarne muttered curses in Swedish.

"I think you all did a fine job," Quill said warmly. "You were under battlefield conditions. The circumstances were unusual, to say the least. And you all tried the best you could. I'm sure of it. And it's my fault Bjarne wasn't here until it was too late. I can't begin to say how sorry I am."

There was a general exhalation, as if all of them had been holding their breath. Kunte wiped his nose and looked a little more cheerful.

"But," Quill said sternly. "Management dereliction—and by management dereliction I mean me—is no excuse for the state of this kitchen. Or the dining room. What happened to the dishwashers and the waiters? Where is everyone else?"

"Their shifts are over at three. I told them they could go a little early," Bjarne said. "Everyone was very upset. The place was a zoo."

"I want everything spotless in half an hour, please," Quill said pleasantly. "This is not a zoo. This is an Inn, one of the finest Inns in upstate New York, and you all should be proud of our ability to handle emergencies like this one. I want the kitchen ready for dinner by four, as usual. We will be open to serve the public at five, as usual. Is that clear? Good. Bjarne? You're in charge of this. Get the dinner shift people in early if you have to. But let's get this done. Kathleen? I think you should go home. I'll give Doreen a call and have her handle the housekeeping until Thursday, okay? That gives you Wednesday to recover yourself a little. I'm so sorry that you had to go through this. If you get your things, I'll walk you out the back door." Quill restrained herself from clapping her hands and yelling, "let's get going, people!" like a particularly obnoxious gym teacher she'd had in high school.

Kathleen fumbled around the bottom of the prep table for her purse. Quill steadied her with one hand. "Peter?" Peter Hairston (who had become an extremely adept sommelier since John Raintree's departure for his own consulting business) dropped a pile of dishes into the wash sink with a clatter. "Ma'am?"

"Kathleen's going to need a ride home. And grab her other side, will you?"

Together they took Kathleen out back to Peter's ancient Volvo. The back lot was almost empty except for Davy Kiddermeister's black-and-white police cruiser and the Hemlock Falls emergency ambulance. Leo's black Lincoln and the stretch Hummer were the only other cars there. Quill was thankful that they hadn't used the front lot; it wouldn't be much longer before the news of Leo's murder hit the village and the sight of crime vehicles was as irresistible to Hemlockians as free beer.

Quill and Peter settled Kathleen into the Volvo's tattered passenger seat. Quill tucked her purse in her lap and smoothed her hair. "Kath?"

"Uh-huh."

"You didn't happen to see the nurse? The one Dina . . . that is the one we called to come and help Mr. Maltby?"

Tears leaked down Kathleen's cheeks. "Did I tell you I quit?"

Quill patted her shoulder. "Of course. I understand. The housekeeping job sucks."

"I saw the nurse," Peter said. He was very young, a med-school dropout who worked at the Inn while deciding what to do with the rest of his life, and the whole debacle had clearly upset him. "I was at the front desk looking for Dina when she came in."

"What did she look like?"

"Look like?" He ran his fingers through his stubbly hair. "Ah. I don't know. She was pretty fat, I guess. Funky glasses."

"Funky how?" Quill interrupted.

"Heart-shaped rims. She had short gray hair. She carried a black bag. And she had a uniform on. White dress. I don't know, Miss Quilliam." He shrugged. "What can I say? She looked like a nurse."

"You didn't recognize her?"

"Me? Nope."

Quill frowned in thought. "Tell me, did she ask you the way to the suite?"

"Nope again. Sorry. Wish I could help."

So she knew the way to the suite. That was significant. "You are helping. Just get Kath back home safe and sound."

"No sweat." He slid into the driver's seat and revved the engine. "I'll be right back."

"Don't rush," Quill urged.

He stuck his head out the window. "Are the cops going to want to talk to me? About my seeing the nurse?"

"I'm headed up there right now. I'll ask."

She waited until the Volvo vanished around the side of the Inn, and then trudged up the fire escape to the third floor fire door. It was locked, as usual. She pulled her master key out of her skirt pocket and let herself in. Her rooms and Meg's suite faced each other at this end of the hall; Leo Maltby's rooms were at the other end. She could see that the door to his suite was open, and she called out as she walked down the hall. "Davy?" Then, recalling Agent Purvis' presence, "Deputy Kiddermeister? It's Quill."

Davy backed out of the open door and waved at her. "Hey, Quill."

"Hey." She stopped in front of him and peered over his shoulder. The suite looked much the same as it had that morning; the table was still drawn up to the couch. Cards lay scattered over the top, and beer bottles were strewn around the carpet. The door to the bedroom was open. Quill caught sight of the EMTs standing in front of the king-size bed.

"We're waiting for forensics," Davy said. "I'd like to go down and check on my sister, but I'd better not leave the scene until somebody else gets here. Is she okay?"

"I asked Peter Hairston to take her home," Quill said.

"I think she's going to be okay, Davy. It was just such a shock."

"First body always is," Davy said. "Not that I hope she ever sees a second."

"I know what you mean. Have you talked to Myles? Is he coming, too?"

Davy raised his eyebrows. "He's in DC. Didn't he tell you? It's how come I had to call the Staties."

"DC!"

"Yeah. I'm sure he left you a message."

Quill patted her pocket for her cell phone. She looked at it in frustration. "It's dead."

Davy took it. "It's not dead, the battery's run down. You have to keep it charged, Quill."

"I know that!" Quill took a deep breath. "Did he say how long he's going to be in DC?"

"Nope. You know how it is with that government job."

Quill knew how it was with that government job. "He probably left a message with Dina, too. But in all the confusion . . . Is there anything I can do? Send up some coffee?"

"You could maybe bring something for Agent Purvis."

"Something? What kind of something?" Quill took a step forward. With a muttered apology, Davy barred the way. "Sorry. Can't let you in just yet. We've got to wait for forensics from Ithaca. He's over there. In the chair by the fireplace."

Quill craned her head around the doorjamb. Agent Purvis sat with his head down between his knees. He was groaning faintly. Davy grinned at her. "He's mostly a desk man, I guess. This is his first body, too. He's a pretty good guy, though, Quill. He didn't have to interrupt his vacation to give us a hand, but he did. And I appreciate it!" he added loudly.

"Agent Purvis is on vacation?"

"Even the FBI gets to take a vacation once in a while."

"Then why did he register under another name!" Quill hissed.

"Why are you upset?"

"I'm not upset. I'm mortified."

"My guess is the poor guy didn't want to be bothered with stuff like this. It's bad enough that he's named after one of the most famous FBI guys around. It's worse that he really is an agent."

Quill made a face. "Oh, dear." This put a monkey wrench into the machinery of her theories for certain. And if the FBI wasn't after Ferris Rodman . . . She sighed heavily. Agent Purvis made a small gulping sound.

Davy lowered his voice to a whisper. "I thought maybe I could send him down to take statements from Mrs. Maltby and the other women, but he said he needed a few minutes to get himself together. But it's been more than a few minutes, Quill. It's been like, half an hour."

"Maybe it's the flu," Quill said charitably.

"Maybe. But I kind of hate to have Lieutenant Parker see him like this." Davy looked at his watch. "The Staties don't like the Feds any more than anyone else—"

"I like the Feds," Quill protested.

"And Parker'll be here soon. It's only half an hour from the state police barracks with the siren on."

Quill had only met one sociopath in her entire life (as far as she knew) and that was State Trooper Parker. She'd encountered Parker several times over the course of her years at the Inn; his flat black gaze and insinuating voice were the stuff of nightmares. She hated Lieutenant Parker the way you hated people like Nicholas Coseque. Only a heartless toad would sic Parker on poor nauseated Mr. Kelvin.

"Why don't you get Agent Purvis to come downstairs with me? I'll put him in my office. We can say he's making phone calls or something."

"I'm fine," Agent Purvis said. He raised his head and got unsteadily to his feet. "I think it was something I had for lunch. The duck. I think it was the duck."

"We haven't had much luck with the duck," Quill said sympathetically. "Would you like to lie down for a bit?"

"I'm on top of it. Really. No need to be concerned."

"Bodies take some folks that way," Davy said helpfully. "Although the deceased looked pretty peaceful, all things considered."

Quill looked at him. "You think he was smothered, then? With the goose-down pillow?"

Davy shrugged. "Early to tell. But the ambulance guys think so."

"Fat." Quill said.

"Huh?"

"Peter said the nurse was fat."

"Pardon me?"

"Nothing. But on the other hand . . . Davy, how many pillows are in the bedroom?"

He pulled his notebook from his pocket. "Three."

"Just three? You're sure?"

"Positive. Two of them were on the floor by the closet and the third one seems to be the weapon. Which is why he looked so good, I guess. Smothering's a pretty peaceful way to go. Now the body in the barn, that was as plain as the nose on your face. Bullet hole right through the back of the skull. Even though almost all of the hair and flesh was burned to a crisp—"

"I think I need to make a few phone calls after all," Agent Purvis said loudly. "Excuse me." He brushed by Quill and jogged down the hall.

"Desk man." Davy said with a regrettable lack of sympathy. "Look. Parker's going to want to talk to Mrs. Maltby. Both Mrs. Maltbys, and those other women, too. Could you get them all in one place for us? And make sure they don't leave?"

"Dina said they were in the Tavern Lounge. I'll go down and make sure they don't have any travel plans." She touched his arm. "I'm sorry Kathleen had to find the body, Davy."

"Me, too. She was all excited about the promotion to housekeeper. Did she tell you she quit?"

Quill took the stairs back down to the main floor. The door to her office was half open, and she could hear Dina chatting away to Agent Purvis. She walked the short hallway that led to the Lounge. Even before she pushed open the door, she could hear the thump of music. As she came through, the music stopped abruptly.

"No, no, NO!" Sheree Maltby shouted. "It's kick and kick and kick and step!"

The low tables and chairs that normally scattered the mahogany floor had been pushed to the far end of the room. Taffi and Candi, dressed in tights, leotards, and running shoes, were standing in the center of the cleared space. Candi mopped her face with a towel. Taffi was bent over, hands on her knees, taking deep breaths. Sheree Maltby stood by a portable CD player with a frown on her face. Brittney-Anne sat in a lounge chair, filing her nails. The table with the CD player on it held bottled water and a litter of Kleenex, purses, makeup, and towels smeared with makeup. At the long mahogany bar, Norrie Ferguson sat with his back to them all. He was nursing a beer, his eyes on the television perched above the shelf that held the liquor.

Sheree punched the CD player and the music thundered through the room. "Again! Kick and kick and kick and . . . Hi! Quill. We were wondering when you'd get here. Dina's about lost her mind."

Quill raised her eyebrows in a "May I" expression and turned the CD player off again. The silence was acute.

Up close, Quill could see that Sheree had been crying, and crying hard. Her eyes were puffy and bloodshot, and the skin on her cheeks was rubbed raw. She blew her nose on a tissue and gave Quill a watery smile. "Nothing like exercise to beat the blues," she said. "How are you, Quill? This is some mess, huh?"

"Nothing like a good slug of vodka to beat the blues," Taffi said. She slung a towel around her neck and tugged at it. "We've been at it over an hour, Sher. What say we knock off and have a drink? Where'd that bartender get to?"

"It's just three o'clock." Sheree said. "Let's wait until the sun's over the yardarm, 'kay?"

"If it's three o'clock, *Days of Ours Lives* is on," Brittney-Anne said languidly.

"There you go, girls. Go turn up that TV." The three younger women drifted off. "And drink some of that water! You don't want to get dehydrated." Sheree sat down with an exhausted sigh. Quill sat across from her. "This is a heck of a thing, isn't it?"

"It is. I'm really sorry."

Sheree shook her head. "Poor Leo. I feel so bad." An indignant shriek diverted her attention. "What!?" she yelled over her shoulder.

"Norrie's watching some stupid truck thing. He won't let us turn to our soaps!"

"Give 'em a break, Norrie! It's a day of loss! You gotta have a little respect!" Sheree turned her attention back to Quill. "Anyway. It's awful to have this happen at your beautiful place."

Quill wasn't sure how to proceed. Sheree was divorced from Leo. And divorced people normally didn't like each other very much. Brittney-Anne was the new Mrs. Maltby and *she* was the one that didn't seem to like Leo very much. Sheree was clearly feeling the effects of Leo's death. And Brittney-Anne . . . Quill turned her head a little to look at the bar. Brittney-Anne was now buffing her nails, rather than filing them. Brittney didn't seem to care at all. "Awful," she echoed. "Awful for all of you."

"Yeah. We all knew Leo was gonna go. But to go like that. I mean, the guy was basically in his prime." She shook her head.

"You knew he was going to die? Had he been receiving death threats?"

"More than usual, you mean?"

Sheree wasn't kidding. She looked at Quill innocently. "He didn't get any death threats that he told me about. It was the way he ate. And the beer. And the cigars. He wasn't as young as he looked, you know. That doctor in Vegas warned him. But Leo wasn't a guy who listened to nobody. Said he'd rather be happy."

A terrible thought rose in Quill's mind. "Um. Sheree. You do know that Leo was—" She faltered. "That his death wasn't natural?"

Sheree's expression was totally blank. "What?"

"The police. That is, you know, um . . . the police. They're looking into it."

"It was his heart." Something fierce flickered in her eyes. "He had a heart attack."

"I'm sorry," Quill said gently. "That isn't true."

Sheree stared at her.

"Look. Can I get you something? Maybe a little

brandy isn't such a bad idea, even though it is early."

"The police don't know anything!"

"Well, I . . ."

"This is a hick town with hick doctors and a hick police force and they don't know a goddam thing!"

Much could and should be forgiven a widow, even if she was the second-best widow, so Quill didn't respond to this provocation.

"You mean they're up there right now? And they think this is a murder?" Quill had never seen anyone wring her hands before. Sheree wrung hers until the skin turned pink.

"I don't understand," Quill said quietly. "They must have told you that the death was suspicious."

Sheree looked at the floor. "I kind of lost it up there, I guess." She looked up. Her expression was troublingly vague. "He's always been there. One way or another. We been through a lot, the two of us." Tears began to roll down her cheeks. She didn't notice them.

Quill wondered if she should give Andy a call.

Sheree sat upright suddenly, as if she'd been stung. "Well, goddam!" She leaned forward and shouted. "Why aren't they out there looking for the guy!?"

"They will be," Quill soothed. "It's just going to take a little time." She took a deep breath. One of the few misgivings she had about detective work was the horrible insensitivity required by good work. "They will want to know what you, Taffi, and Candi were doing this afternoon. If you can let me know where you were, it might speed the investigation up a little bit. It will help catch whomever it was that did this."

Sheree didn't seem to take this in, at first. "Where we were? All three of us? We were together in the Village. At that little gift shop. Adela's Bella Boutique."

"Was Brittney-Anne with you"

"What's going on?" Norrie Ferguson stood over them, his thumbs hooked into the loops of his white sharkskin pants. "What's wrong, Sher?"

"She says Leo didn't pass away in his sleep! She says somebody got up there and killed him!"

Norrie shook his head.

"You knew?!"

"Well, Sher, I had a word with that kid deputy. . . ."

"You knew and you didn't tell me."

"I figured it'd just upset you," Norrie said feebly.

"No kidding!" she flung herself backwards in the chair. "It's one thing when God takes a person because it's that person's time. It's another goddam thing when somebody does it on purpose."

"You're right about that, Sher."

"Does this mean we're stuck in the boonies?" Taffi asked. She and Candi had wandered over, the soap opera forgotten. Brittney-Anne had wandered over, too. But she hadn't forgotten about buffing her fingernails, although she suspended the activity to listen. "And what about the funeral?" Taffi said. She pushed at her flaming-red hair. "You told us we'd have a really terrific funeral."

"Yeah, this means we're stuck in the boonies," Brittney-Anne said contemptuously.

Sheree jumped out of her chair and began to pace up and down. She was crying again.

Brittney-Anne tucked her nail buffer into a makeup pack on the table and withdrew a tiny cell phone. "It also means we've got to get ourselves a lawyer and the whole bit."

"A lawyer?" Candi blinked. "What kind of lawyer is going to come all the way out here?"

"You don't need a lawyer," Norrie said. "You didn't do anything."

Brittney-Anne's gaze flicked contemptuously over him. "Think about it, dickhead. Three strippers and a has-been goon." She gave Norrie a contemptuous look. Her pink tongue flickered over her lips. "Leo used to say you look like you'd been rode hard and put away wet, Sher. I don't care what you wanna call these two or yourself, for that matter. You're ex-hookers and you look like hookers. And I'm not so sure that these two are all that ex, if you get my meaning." She looked smug and mean. "Anyhow, if you think this town's gonna try to pin this murder on who really did it you're dumber than you look. And that's pretty dumb. The four of us are smack in the middle of this thing. So I'm calling the best lawyer I can find, and I'm going to tell him to get his flippin' butt over here as fast as his little legs can carry him. *Capice?*" She turned her back, walked off, and punched numbers into her cell phone.

Candi pinched Sheree on the arm. "You said we could get out of here as soon as we got Leo to the mortuary."

"I guess I was wrong."

"Forget it." Candi crouched down and began to stuff towels, makeup, and water bottles into a tote bag. "I'm getting out of here. And if you have any sense, you'll come with me. Brittney-Anne's right. They are going to try to pin this on us, and we're suckers if we stick around for it." She stood up and tossed her head so that her black hair rippled down her shoulders. "Sorry. But we gave it our best shot, Sher. I mean, reform's a great idea and all that, but reform's for suckers. And this girl's no sucker."

Taffi nodded vigorously. "Gotcha." She picked up her purse.

"Well, ladies. Headed back to the streets? Not yet, if you don't mind. Not just yet."

Quill didn't have to turn to identify that oily voice. "Hello, Lieutenant Parker."

"Miss . . . Quilliam." Parker was short. Not so short that he failed the height requirements for New York State Troopers, but short enough so that he looked directly into Quill's eyes when he stood close to her, which is what he did now. His hair was dark, thin, and oily. His skin was a peculiar texture—large-pored and thick—that made Quill's own skin crawl in revulsion.

Sheree pushed herself between Quill and Parker with sharp jabs of her elbows. "Who are you?"

His reptilian eyes flickered over her contemptuously. "Police."

"You're here about Leo?"

"I'm here about some piece of slime that got offed

upstairs. That who you mean by 'Leo'?"

Sheree shoved her face into Parker's and hissed. "You listen to me you little creep. It's 'Mr. Maltby' to you."

"Got hold of Ken Brandstetter," Brittney-Anne said, stepping to Sheree's side. She held the cell phone up. "Wanna say 'hi' creep? He'd like to listen in on this chat we're having. And you don't have to speak up." She held her phone to her ear. "Yep. He can hear just fine." She crowded Parker on the left.

"Lawyered up already?" Parker sneered.

"You've heard of him?" Taffi asked. She and Candi stood shoulder to shoulder with Sheree and crowded Parker on the right. "Mr. Brandstetter?"

"He has little apes like you," Brittney-Anne tapped Parker insolently with one long nail, "for breakfast."

CHAPTER 12

"You should have been there," Quill marveled. "I couldn't believe it. The four of them just sneered Parker out the door. It was amazing."

John Raintree set his glass of Syrah on the table and nodded in agreement. It was after seven, and Quill was treating both of them to a full course meal in the dining room. The light was soft, and it made John's bronze skin even bronzer. He was Onondaga Indian on his mother's side, and Quill thought he was one of the handsomest men she'd ever met. "It sounds amazing. But Parker's got a bad rep. You should watch your step with him, Quill."

"I always do. Although I have to admit, the name of the lawyer Brittney-Anne called intimidated him more than anything else. Even I've heard of him. Anyway . . ." She reached across the table and clasped John's hands between hers. "I'm so glad you're here tonight! I didn't think you'd be able to get here until the day of the wedding."

"I was happy to clear my schedule. And yes, I can stay for the rest of the week. But Quill, as good as it is to see you, it's not like you to be overwhelmed." He paused, appeared to rethink this, and then said, "Let's put it this way. Although I'm always ready to help whenever you need me, for whatever you need me, it's not like you to call for help. Is there something going on I should know about?"

Quill left her revelation for the third course, which was a creamy mushroom risotto that was going to put John in a very good mood. "Well, there is, but it'll keep."

She was feeling relaxed for the first time all day. When John had left his position as her business manager to open his own business, he had agreed to stay on as their tax accountant, which meant that she still saw him once a month. But it wasn't the same as their day-to-day meetings. It was good to see him just for that. It was even better that his help in the next few days was going to give her the time she needed to solve Leo Maltby's murder. She'd already put a call into Adela to check the whereabouts of the Boom-Boom girls that afternoon. Their alibi had been confirmed. "How's the duck?"

John looked at his plate judiciously. "Jerry's recipe," he said. "It's great."

"Doreen called Jerry back. I told you about that, didn't I? That he was um, called away unexpectedly this morning?" Quill ate some of the duck. She didn't mention that Jerry had suggested tranquilizers before he came back to run Meg's kitchen. Not for him, but for Quill. Somebody really needed to talk to Meg. She was driving the poor guy crazy. "So Jerry's back to give Bjarne a hand, for which I am well and truly grateful. It would have been tough to pull the wedding off without him. It would be impossible to pull it off without you."

"So it's still on, is it?"

Quill straightened in alarm. "What do you mean, is it still on? Of course it's still on! Who told you it wasn't on? Meg? Have you been talking to Meg?"

The clatter in the dining room stilled. As Quill had expected, the news of Leo Maltby's murder had increased business at the Inn, rather than driven people away. Quill clapped her hand over her mouth and muttered, "Sorry."

If John were surprised at Quill's sudden vehemence, he didn't show it. "I just wondered. In light of all the activity surrounding Maltby's death, it wouldn't surprise me if you decided to put it off for a while. It's not a large wedding, you said."

"The wedding, no. It's about the size of your wedding to Lisa. It's just Andy's mother and father and his brother. And then our side. Which is you and Doreen and Dina." Quill waved her hands. "That's about it. Our niece, Corisande, is in Italy with Aunt Eleanor. They can't come, because Eleanor's off on assignment in Africa the day after tomorrow. But they sent a beautiful carved mask for a present. You know. I'm not even sure if Myles can make it. He's still stuck in DC."

Myles had left a message for her. More than one. She really was going to have to get a better grip on the use of her cell phone.

"The reception's another matter but we're used to big parties, of course. All of the Inn staff will come and the Chamber, too." She made a face. "At least, I think most of them are coming. They wouldn't boycott Meg's wedding just because they're mad at me, would they? And now that poor Leo Maltby's dead, no one has to worry about the strip joint." She put her fork down. Suddenly, even Jerry's duck didn't appeal to her.

John's left eyebrow quirked upward. "I just wondered if the presence of the troopers, an FBI agent, reporters from all of the local television stations, three strippers—"

"They aren't strippers, John."

"They aren't?" He turned and looked at table 27, the one by the waterfall, where Sheree, Taffi, and Candi were eating Jerry's duck. They were dressed in a more subdued manner than usual, either out of respect for Leo or because Quill knew for a fact that Angela Stoner had refused to interview them on live TV unless they put tee-shirts over the sequined bras. All three were in (very) short metallic skirts and tank tops that only exposed a few inches of midriff. Someone had allowed

Max into the dining room, and Taffi was feeding him bits of bread.

"Well, yes, they do have plans to go on *Oprah* after this is all over and give the audience lessons in taking their clothes off. Sheree's excited about that. But they're human beings, John. Women just trying to make it in a tough, tough world. This case is so unfair. Brittney-Anne was right: everyone does think they killed Leo. Which is why I have to have the next two days free to solve this murder. For them. So that they can get on with their lives. That's why I called you."

There. It was out. And he hadn't even had the mushroom risotto. Quill sat back, and said in a lower tone of voice, "Of course, *you* understand why I have to do this. It's justice."

A very faint smile crossed John's face. "Who *doesn't* understand why you have to do this?"

"Myles, of course."

"Myles probably has as much compassion for the lot of those women as I do. Which means, as usual, he isn't happy with your career as Sarah Quilliam, Private Eye."

Quill looked at him in a very dignified way. "I don't take any money for what I do, John. I feel very strongly about giving back what I can to the community."

John coughed. Hard. Quill wondered if she should pat him on the back, then decided against it. Because if John laughed the same way he coughed, with his hand over his mouth and his head down, and if he were laughing at her, she didn't want to know about it.

John's smile was warm. "Is there anything you'd like me to take care of first?"

"I'm afraid the reservations are in a bit of a mess," she apologized. "And I haven't gotten to this month's bills. And did I tell you that we don't have a housekeeper? And that Meg makes periodic forays into the kitchen to sabotage Jerry?" She waved her hand in the air. "You know. Just the usual."

She spent longer over coffee with John than she'd intended. He let drop, in his diffident way, that Lisa was pregnant. She was fine, he said, they were both very happy, and by the time Quill had called Lisa and exchanged delighted shrieks, it was almost ten o'clock, and she was aware of her own profound fatigue. She made her way to the third floor ready to drop, Max padding at her heels.

Her rooms had never seemed so welcoming. It was quiet. Blissfully quiet. And except for the clothes she'd dropped on the floor the night before, when she'd come back from the visit to Seasons in the Sun, the place was wonderfully clean and neat. Quill bent to pick them up. She was tired of chaos and mess and noise.

The wig.

The gray wig was gone.

"Max," she said. "This might be easier to solve then I thought. But remember Nero Wolfe's advice to Archie Godwin: never theorize in advance of the facts." She sat down on her bed, thinking. If she just weren't so tired.

She hadn't yet looked at the results of Dina's Google search on Antonia Caprese and Leo, which was still sitting in her office. She tramped downstairs again, retrieved the papers, and hauled herself back. They really needed to put in an elevator.

Outside her own door, she hesitated. She'd seen Meg briefly earlier that evening: the house in Covert was a dump, Andy had an emergency at the clinic, and how come Quill had let Leo Maltby get murdered right upstairs in broad daylight? After unloading, Meg had flounced upstairs and locked herself in her room.

"What do you think, Max?"

Max sat down and yawned heartily.

"I'm pooped, too. Which is an advantage, because I'm too tired to wring her neck, which is what I want to do after that stunt she pulled this morning."

Max rolled over and wriggled, scratching his back on the carpeting.

"Stop that. And she's always, *always* helped solved these cases before."

Max gave her a puzzled glance, then pawed at her shoe.

The door to Meg's rooms cracked open, and her sister poked her head out. "Oh," she said. "It's you. And my dog." She backed up and swung the door all the way open. "Come in."

Meg's private space was very different from her own. One wall was painted persimmon. Plants flourished everywhere. At the moment, boxes of her cookbooks were scattered around the lemon-colored carpeting in the living room; when Meg was in permanent residence, cookbooks were scattered unboxed all over the floor. Max flopped down the middle of a low-lying pile of books and went to sleep.

Meg's rooms overlooked the front lawn and the waterfall, and she had placed a peacock blue sectional in front of her French doors to take advantage of the view. The doors were open to the soft August air. Quill picked her way through the clutter and stepped out onto the balcony. A quarter moon sailed in the sky, veiled now and again by passing clouds. She couldn't see the falls, but she could hear them.

Meg spoke at her elbow. "Taffi—or maybe it was Candi, I can't tell them apart—anyhow, she thinks we should put klieg lights at the base of the falls. Like they do in Vegas."

"Speaking of Vegas, Ferris Rodman wants to open a gambling casino at the Resort."

"You're kidding me!"

"Nope." Quill wandered back inside. Meg's wedding dress hung on the outside of the bedroom door. Quill had picked it out herself. Meg had gray eyes and the clear, translucent complexion of their Welsh ancestors. She looked wonderful in crystal pastels, and the dress was a soft gray silk overshot with rose. She fingered the fabric absentmindedly, then sat down on the couch. "I told you about the gambling last March. Remember? Marge and I found the application for a license in his construction office."

"Oh, yeah. The time you tried solving crimes without

me." Meg sat next to her. "I thought that idea disappeared along with the small boutique hotel he was going to put up in the Civil War Cemetery."

"To be perfectly accurate, Marge and I think that Rodman wants to go ahead with it. We don't have any actual proof. But now . . ."

"Hm. Do you think it's connected to all this other stuff? The body in the barn? Leo Maltby's murder?"

Quill looked down at the sheaf of papers in her hand. "It must be. Otherwise none of this makes much sense."

"Oh, I can think of several alternative theories to the crime," Meg said wisely.

"You can, huh? Like what?"

Meg waved her hand in the air. "Give me a minute. I'll think of something. What kind of evidence do we have?"

Quill was getting her second wind. "I haven't had time to sit down and sort it all out. I was planning on doing that tonight. Do you want to help?"

"Of course I want to help. Haven't you always been my Watson?"

"I'm Holmes. You're Watson."

"Whatever." She nudged Quill companionably. "Sure. My last case before I depart for the land of the happily wedded. What's that pile of stuff? This month's bills that you haven't had time to pay because I've been a complete and total jerk to you?"

Quill scowled. Detection could wait. "You have been a complete and total jerk to me. What the heck is going on?"

Meg edged away, then curled herself around a throw pillow. It was lemon-colored, like the carpet. Quill didn't like bright colors when she was tired. They shouted at her. "Well?"

"I'm thinking."

"How can you think in here, anyway?" she asked crossly. "It's too noisy."

"Don't be cross with me, Quill. And I don't need a lecture, thank you very much."

"I'm not cross with you. But it's time for a talk."

"Anytime you're mad at me, that's exactly what you say: it's time for a talk. And then you lecture me."

"Since when!"

"Since I was twelve years old, when Mom and Dad died." Meg threw the pillow on the floor.

Quill was silent.

"You were sixteen years old when you started to take care of me. That was more than twenty years ago. I'm grown up, Quill. It's time to stop."

"I'll stop when you start acting like a grown up."

"I'm thirty-four years old!" Meg shrieked. "And I don't need a mother!"

Max sat up and began to bark. Somebody pounded on Meg's front door. Quill grabbed a second throw pillow (a nice, uncomplicated beige) and put it over her head.

Meg stamped to the door, threw it open, and demanded, "What!?"

"Heard all the noise. Just wondered if the girls were in here." Norrie Ferguson stepped inside. He looked rotten. His long, lugubrious face was even longer and more lugubrious than it had been that afternoon.

"Just come right in, Mr. Ferguson," Meg said sarcastically.

"Meg," Quill protested. "What can we do for you, Norrie? You're looking for the Boom-Boom girls, I take it?"

"Yeah. I had this idea. You seen 'em?"

"The last I saw of them, they were in the dining room," Quill said. "They left around eight or so. I think they were headed to the Croh Bar."

"Then they'll be awhile. Mind if I have a seat? Maybe I could bounce it off you two. See what you think?" His eyes were hopeful. And lonely. "Used to bounce ideas off Leo all the time. Can't do that now, of course."

"We'd love to hear about your idea. Actually, I'd like to talk with you about what happened this afternoon, too. Maybe we could have a nice discussion about all of it." She gave Meg a meaningful glance. Meg nodded in instant understanding, picked up a note pad and perched on the arm of the couch, all attention.

Quill smiled warmly at Norrie. What better place to begin her investigation than with the man who'd practically seen the whole thing? She patted the space next to her. "Please sit down. This must have been a terrific shock to you."

Norrie sat down with a heavy thud. "Who would have thought Leo'd buy the farm the way he did?"

"I'm so sorry. You two must go back a long way."

"Oh, yeah. Before Miranda."

"Miranda who?" Meg asked, pencil poised.

"You know, the read-'em-their-rights law. Things got a lot easier after Miranda. 1965," he added reminiscently. "Yeah. We go back a good bit. I mean, we did."

"Very hard on you," Quill murmured. "Now, about this afternoon, Norrie. Did you leave the suite at any time before Dina came up to call the nurse?"

"Leave? No. We were in the middle of a game. Poker. Besides, where would I go? I was supposed to stick with Leo."

"Did anyone come to the suite other than Dina in that time?"

"Uh. Coffee came up. For Brittney-Anne."

"Brittney-Anne," Quill said. "Uh-huh. When did she leave the suite?"

"How'd you know she left?"

Quill looked wise. "She did, didn't she?"

"Yeah. Just after that cute kid from downstairs made the call to the nursing service. Went out for a jog, she said."

"A jog, huh." Quill nodded. "And she didn't get back until after the nurse had gone."

"Wow," Meg said, "do you mean what I think you mean?"

Quill held up her hand and ticked each point off on her finger. "One: my gray wig is missing. Two: it is *highly* significant that the nurse showed up within twenty minutes of that phone call. You don't get service that fast from McDonald's. Three: *cui bono?* Who benefits from poor Leo's death? The widow, of course, and Brittney-Anne said as much this afternoon. 'At least the old fart left me enough to live on'. And fourth: Peter said the nurse was fat. Did you count the pillows in 321? Two of the goose down pillows are missing. We know where one is—in the forensics lab in Ithaca. The other was used to make a size-six stripper look like a size-sixteen nurse."

Norrie had been following this conversation the way tennis buffs follow a match. "Hold on, girls. You think that bimbo Brittney-Anne had something to do with this?"

"Please don't use that term with us," Meg said crisply.

"Sorry. Sheree don't like to be called bimbo, either."

"Not that. Brittney-Anne *is* a bimbo. It's girls. Don't call us girls."

Norrie looked even more confused. "You mean, you two had that operation? Jeezola. I never woulda guessed it."

"Stop," Quill said. " 'Girls' is a term that should refer to any female under twelve, Mr. Ferguson. We are women."

"Right. Okay, then. I wouldn't put it past that bi—that gi—what the heck you want me to call her? Anyways, she got back from the jog before the nurse left. Raised holy hell about getting kicked out of the suite. Made us wait while she took a shower!"

"She was there while the nurse was there?" Quill said, dismayed.

Meg crossed out everything that she'd written down and said, "Nice going, Watson."

"I mean, her and Leo had their fights, sure. But she loves, him, ya know? Fact."

Quill patted his hand. "I'm sure she does. Did." She turned to Meg. "Back to Rodman."

"Rodman?"

"The next logical suspect, of course."

"I need a glass of wine," Meg said. She went into her small kitchen and Quill heard her open her refrigerator.

"You got a beer in there, I wouldn't mind it," Norrie called out. "So, about this idea I got. Like I said, I figure it'd be a good idea to bounce it off you two."

Meg returned with two glasses of red wine and a bottle of Grolsch.

"No Bud?" Norrie asked hopefully.

"That's horse piddle," Meg said. "Try that." She set the beer on her coffee tablc. "So where were we?"

"I thought about calling 'em the Flipping Ferguson Four!" Norrie said loudly.

Quill almost spilled her wine. It was a Mouton Cadet and it wouldn't have improved the color of Meg's carpet.

"Women," Norrie said to the ceiling, "sometimes you just got to shout to get their attention."

"Calling who what?" Meg eyed him over the rim of her wineglass.

"I can't call them the Boom-Boom girls anymore now that Leo's gone toes. The Flipping Ferguson Four has a little more class." Norrie raised his beer. "Headliner," he explained.

"Flipping?" Meg said.

Norrie twirled his hands on front of his chest.

Quill set her wineglass down carefully. "You mean Lovejoy's Nudie Bar and Grill is still a . . . a viable concern?"

"And what's that when it's at home?"

"You mean you're going to convert MacAvoy's barn to a strip joint?"

Norrie laughed, heh-heh-heh. "Put a class joint like that in this hick town? No offense, Quill. No way in hell."

"I am quite offended, actually," Quill said.

"We don't want a strip joint," Meg said.

"Of course we don't. But this town's good enough for a strip joint. Any strip joint."

"That's true. Please don't call us a hick town, either, Norrie."

"But . . . never mind. Anyways, Leo never meant to put it here. Just thought he'd get a little extra financing out of Rodman. Although it *was* weird, now that I think about it." He thought about it. It was obviously very hard work. "Nah. He wouldna."

"I *told* you," Quill said. "It's back to Rodman."

"You mean you were blackmailing Ferris Rodman?" Meg said. "Threatening to blow his plans for an upscale casino, perhaps?"

"No flies on you, kiddo. And it wasn't no blackmail. Blackmail's illegal. We were just sellin' the license. I'm the one takin' offense now, if you get my drift." Norrie didn't look as if he'd stepped out of the pages of a Damyon Runyon novel anymore. He looked more like a character out of Jeffery Deaver.

"Did it work?" Quill asked. "The wholly legitimate offer to sell the license to Ferris Rodman?"

"Gave us a lousy first offer, didn't he?" Norrie said. "A hundred K. We wanted half a mil. So he insults us, and follows it up by that thumping in the parking lot. And of course that didn't work. Leo's been thumped by better guys than that, and so have I. On top of that, Rodman called the suite this morning to tell us the 'offer was withdrawn.'" Norrie was actually pretty good at imitating Rodman's low-key tones. "Thought he was bluffing, myself." He hunched forward. "But I'll tell ya. This is what I was thinking about before."

"You mean just a few minutes ago?" Meg said. "That's what you were doing."

"Meg!"

"I got the distinct feeling Leo really liked it here."

"I don't think Rodman was bluffing," Quill said slowly.

"Unless . . . Norrie, what time did that call come in?"

"How the hell am I supposed to remember that? It was after Sheree and the girls left, that's all I know."

And how is Mr. Maltby this morning?

And she was the one who told the cold-blooded murderer Leo needed a nurse. "I knew the guy was dangerous," Quill said aloud.

"Who? Rodman?" Norrie snorted. "Anybody can send out a few gazooks to thump a guy when he's not looking." Was that the price of a man's life? A license to run a topless bar?

But the referendum would have taken care of Maltby's plans anyway. And there was that look on Rodman's face when Harvey proposed it. Was there something more than money at stake here? Quill tugged at her hair.

"Norrie," she began.

"This beer ain't bad, Meg," he said. "You got another?"

"Sure."

"Norrie. Do you know somebody named Caprese?"

"Never heard of her," he said automatically. He shot his cuff and looked at his watch. It was a 24-carat gold Rolex. "Better get my ass in gear and go looking for those girls. Women, I mean. Save the beer for another time, Meg." He got up, knocking the papers in Quill's lap to the floor in the process. "Sorry. Ma always said I was a size ten foot in a size twelve shoe. Thanks for the gab fest, ladies." He stacked the papers roughly together and handed them back to her. "So. I'm outta here. Ciao!"

"Ciao," Meg said. She shut the door after him and came back to her perch on the couch.

"You noticed, of course."

"Noticed what?"

"How he beat feet the minute I mentioned the body."

"I did."

"Did I say Antonia Caprese? I did not. I said 'Caprese.'"

"And he said, 'never heard of her.'"

"So how did he know she was a woman?"

"I don't know. How?"

Quill just looked at her. "Meg! Wake up here! Did I tell you about Leo's gold lighter?"

"The one that convinced you it was Leo's body in the MacAvoy barn? Everyone knows about the gold lighter, Quill."

"I think Leo was there."

"I'm sure you're right."

"And I think Leo killed her."

"You're probably right about that, too. But does it matter now? Leo's dead."

"Of course it matters. We need to know who Antonia Caprese was. If we know that, we can find out why Leo killed her. Which should lead us to . . ."

"Who killed Leo?" Meg yawned so widely her jaw cracked. "Can we not do this now? I'm exhausted. I'm so exhausted I'm going to sleep standing up."

"It's not that late. It's just after eleven. You used to be such a night owl."

"I'm considering that operation."

"What operation?"

"The one to turn me into a lark. Not the one Norrie thought we had to turn ourselves into men."

Quill shuddered. "The guy is just weird. This case is getting to have a very bad feel to it."

"You need to sleep, too." Meg got behind her and began pushing her out of the living room. Max got up and shuffled after them. "Go to bed. And don't come bothering me with any brilliant ideas you get in the middle of the night. Okay? We'll talk about this in the morning."

Quill riffled through the printouts. "I can't stand not knowing what's in here. How can you?"

"It'll keep, that's why." Meg glanced at her watch and said impatiently, "Come on. Quill. Please go to bed. You look like a zombie."

"Fine."

"Fine."

Quill and Max went back to her rooms. She took a shower, got into her nightgown, and got into bed. She spread the closely printed sheets out in front of her.

There were a few newspaper stories about Leo. He'd been arrested for various criminal activities that were usually associated with the Mob. But the really interesting information was on Antonia Caprese.

Quill read it. Then she retrieved her notebook that held her notes on the Chamber meeting and looked at the parade route for the protest march. She picked up the phone to call Myles. She put the phone back down again, and thought about what she should do in the morning.

She woke once in the night, knowing that someone was in the room with her.

"Myles?"

But it wasn't Myles.

CHAPTER 13

"How in the heck do you get yourself into this kind of trouble all the time?" Doreen's face loomed over her. She looked like an angry chicken.

Quill tried to sit up. "Ow! Oh, my head!" Then she became aware of an even more urgent problem. "Doreen!"

"Here." Doreen thrust a stainless steel bowl under her nose. Quill vomited neatly into the bowl. "Lay back, then."

She sank back against something soft and shut her eyes. "I have the worst headache I've ever had in my life. I'm wrong. I have the worst headache of the century."

"Doesn't stop you from talkin' a blue streak, does it?"

Quill opened her eyes again. She was in her own bedroom. That was good. The nausea overcame her again. Doreen provided a new, clean bowl, for which Quill was profoundly thankful.

"Are you sure she shouldn't be in the hospital?" That was Meg.

"I'm sure. She'll start to feel better in a couple of hours."

"Hi, Andy." Her voice was disgustingly feeble. "What happened to me?"

"Do you remember anything at all about last night?"

"Myles is back?" Memory came flooding, and she sat up. She regretted it immediately.

"For heaven's *sake,*" Meg snapped. "Why are you trying to make her guess? I found you on the floor of your living room, sweetie. There was a towel over your mouth soaked with chloroform. It turned out to be chloroform, that is. I didn't realize it at the time."

"Somebody chloroformed me," Quill said. It wasn't a question. She remembered a confused struggle. And she had tried to run for the door. She hadn't made it.

Doreen put a cold cloth on her face. "Thanks," she said through the folds. "Helps to keep my eyes closed."

"Davy said there'd been a break-in at Dr. McKenzie's place last night," Meg continued angrily. "You know, the veterinarian down near Ithaca? I don't know why the old geek had it lying around, but he did."

"Max?"

"Some watch dog *he* is. He didn't bark. But there's a nice ham bone slobbering up the corner of your kitchen. I guess he was too busy stuffing his face to raise the alarm."

Max poked a cold nose into her hand. Quill imagined it was apologetic. It was more likely he was looking for food. Quill, not sure of who else was in her room, didn't say anything more. She wondered how long it would take to be able to keep her eyes open without the need to throw up. "Are there any clues lying around?"

"What? Clues? You mean as to who did this to you? Well, those printouts Dina made for us are gone. Which is totally stupid, because if that's what they were after, all we have to do is Google them again. And forget about Rodman, Quill. I know for a fact he went to Syracuse yesterday afternoon for the night. He took Andy with him, except Andy came back. He wants a doctor on call for the Resort and Andy helped him interview."

"Whoever it was wanted to know what was in there," Quill said. "The printouts."

"Norrie Ferguson was the only person outside of us who knew you had those printouts. He helped you pick them up. You think he did this to you?"

"I don't know, Meg," she said evasively. She took a deep breath. "I can't think about it right now. My head feels like all seventy-six trombones in the last act of *The Music Man.*"

Andy murmured something. Quill couldn't quite catch it. "What?" she demanded.

"We're going to let you rest for a bit. Try to sleep. Andy says you'll feel better in four hours or so."

"What time is it now?

"About five o'clock. In the morning."

"I'm gonna sleep on the couch." Doreen's voice brooked no argument about that. Quill knew why Doreen was at the Inn at five o'clock in the morning; Stoke had a police scanner in their house so that he could catch any fast-breaking news.

"And I'll be right across the hall." Meg's hand fumbled for hers and squeezed it. "Jeez. I thought you were dead."

"I wish I were."

"I'm going to go pound Norrie Ferguson with a meat mallet. And then I'm going to feed him to the pigs."

"It wasn't Norrie."

"Who else could it have been? Who else knew about the printouts?"

"We'll take care of it later, Meg. Honest. Is Davy racing around arresting people?"

"He wanted to talk to you first."

"Tell him to back off, okay?"

"Are you sure?"

"I'm sure."

She didn't think it was possible, given the way she was feeling, but she drifted off to sleep. When she woke again, sunlight flooded the room and her headache was a dim pounding in the back of her skull. She pushed herself upright and sat on the edge of the bed. The carpeting swam before her eyes. "Bleah," she said. "This is ridiculous."

"How ya doin'?"

Quill looked up and smiled. Doreen stood at the open door. She held a tray with a pot of tea on it. "I can't believe how thirsty I am."

"Yeah, well don't gulp it, now. You don't want to barf it all over the bedspread."

"I see lemon, too. Thanks." Quill stood up. The room didn't spin.

"You just lay back, there."

"I'll feel better if I move around a bit." She took a couple of deep breaths. "Let's have the tea in the kitchen."

"I'm gonna change you out of that nightgown first."

Quill looked down at herself. "Yuck." She allowed Doreen to draw the nightgown over her head, and felt much better after she'd put on a fresh tee-shirt and a pair of her oldest jeans. Doreen guided her into the living room and settled her on the couch. "You sit," she ordered. "And I'll make you some scrambled eggs."

"Honestly, Doreen, I can't. The tea's fine."

"You sure?"

"Very sure."

"That Davy's waitin' to see you as soon as you feel up to it."

"Can he wait a little longer, do you think? The last time I felt like this I'd drunk half a bottle of blackberry brandy in college. I'll be fine. It'll just take awhile. Sit down for a minute."

Doreen sat down next to her. She was wearing pedal pushers and a worn cotton blouse.

"You've got your housekeeping clothes on today. You're not quitting on me, too, are you?"

Doreen lowered her chin. "Who else is quittin' on you?"

"Kathleen, Bjarne, and Dina all quit. Everybody I promoted wants to go straight back to the jobs they held two days ago." Quill hiccupped. "Maybe I need to take another one of those management courses at the Cornell University Extension School. I didn't do this properly."

Doreen scowled fiercely. "You did good. I just don't think I'm cut out for the job of tour director. Looks like the guests I got to come in are no good. That Norrie Ferguson tried to kill you." To Quill's absolute horror, Doreen's eyes filled with tears.

"Doreen, if you start to cry, I'll start to cry. Don't. Please. Pinch your knee."

She pinched her knee, grinned, and blew her nose. "Anyways. As soon as you feel up to it, I'm getting' that Davy and he'll throw that Ferguson fella right into jail where he belongs."

"Norrie Ferguson didn't try to kill me," Quill said patiently. "If he had, he would have shot me in the back of the neck."

Doreen's black eyes brightened. "You mean he killed that Caprese character?"

"No, I think I know why Leo Maltby killed Antonia Caprese. It's why he's dead and not Norrie. Except Norrie hasn't figured it out yet. When he does, he'll be out of here like a shot. Even if he has seen those computer printouts, he may not catch on right away. He's not the smartest duck in the flock." Quill leaned back against the couch. She wished she didn't feel as if she'd been run over by a tractor trailer. It made it harder to keep things straight. "What I haven't quite figured is why Leo was killed."

"You know who did him, too?" Doreen was impressed.

"I think so," Quill said cautiously. "But the evidence is gone. It has to be. The murderer is too smart to keep it around. And that means there's no way Myles can prove it."

"If there's no evidence, how do you know who done it?" Doreen said skeptically.

"When Meg and I got to the site of the fire that

morning, Elmer said he'd gotten a phone call about the fire around four in the morning from a man who didn't identify himself. That didn't strike me as significant at the time. But later at the Chamber meeting, Elmer was convinced that Leo had left town. He was very upset that he hadn't. That's the first clue I had about who Leo's murderer is. And Myles told me that Antonia Caprese had been killed somewhere else. I think Leo's killer brought the body to Leo so they could dispose of it. That's why the fire was set. But Leo's killer has been playing both ends against the middle. That's why he called Elmer when the fire started. I think he told Elmer something like 'Maltby set that fire to conceal a crime. You make sure that an investigation's started.' He'd told Elmer about the plans for the strip joint, you see, and Elmer was terrified that the town was going to pitch a fit. Which it did. But Leo didn't leave town. And Elmer was too chicken to speak up.

"Anyhow, that's what started me thinking about who killed Leo." Quill sat lost in thought. She got up suddenly and headed to the bathroom.

"You okay? You gonna barf again?"

"I'm fine. I'm going to wash my face and comb my hair. Doreen, could you do me a big favor? Could you not mention this to anyone? I need to see Sheree Maltby. I just hope Davy's on top of it, and that the Boom-Boom girls haven't left town."

"Sheree?"

"Yes. Have you seen her this morning?"

"Not yet. Far as I know, they're sleepin' in. Mike tells me they got back real late last night."

Sheree tapped tentatively at Quill's door about twenty minutes later.

"Come in!" Quill called. She was seated at her small kitchen table with a second pot of tea. "Would you like some tea?"

"Jeez, kiddo. You look like something the cat dragged in." Sheree's smile was as tentative as her knock. She was dressed in workout gear, but her makeup was as thickly applied as Quill had ever seen it. "Word is you got mugged in your own living room." She screwed up her face. Then she dropped into the chair opposite Quill's. "It's like you're not safe anywhere these days. I'm really sorry." Max padded over and nudged her hand with his nose. "Hey, Maxie," she said. She scratched his ears affectionately. "How's it hangin, bud?"

Quill looked at her over the rim of her teacup. "He's hoping you have another ham bone for him."

Sheree's smile flashed. "He likes ham, huh?"

Quill didn't say anything, just regarded her steadily.

"Well, I just dropped in to see how you were doing, honey. And to thank you for being so nice to us here. As soon as that cute little deputy gives us the word, we're out of here. Did you hear about *Oprah*?" Her smile flashed again, this time with genuine excitement. "Can you believe it? Us four on TV? The Boom would be over the moon about this."

"It's a shame Tonia can't be there with you," Quill said. Sheree's smile remained fixed in place.

"You and Antonia Caprese were the two original Boom-Boom girls, weren't you? Leo even got you two booked in Las Vegas as an opening act."

Her words wiped all the expression from Sheree's face. "So?" she said after a long moment. "anybody could of found that out."

"That's right, anyone could have. And the police undoubtedly will. And that was all that was in the computer printouts, Sheree. What I'm wondering is what you *thought* I had."

Sheree chewed her lower lip.

"I think what you thought I had was proof of some link between Leo and his killer."

Quill waited. Sometimes waiting was the best tactic of all. Sheree began picking nervously at her nails.

"I've figured most of it out. Even the chloroform. You must have visited the vet when Tooey got sick."

Sheree gave a slight nod.

"And then you went back last night to find something to knock me out?" Quill smiled. "I hear Dr. MacKenzie's quite a character. I take Max to the small-animal clinic here in town and I haven't met him. Did you like him?"

"The town vet was on vacation," Sheree said, "and he was taking her calls for her." Her face got wistful. "He sure thinks a lot of that wife of his. You should see them together. He's gotta be a hundred and three if he's a day and she's as fat as a house and don't the sun shine out of her rear end."

"He loves her."

"Yeah. Like Leo and I loved each other." She looked sternly at Quill. "He made a mistake, the day he married Brittney-Anne. I knew it in my bones. It was just a matter of time. Leo's always been a fool for good looks. They were already talking about a whatdyacallit . . . separation."

"An amicable separation?"

"She's headed off for the big time anyway," Sheree said. "If I'd looked like that at twenty-two, Leo said I would have been a headliner at Vegas four times over. Anyhow. It's like I said. It was only a matter of time."

"I don't quite understand how Antonia came into this," Quill said gently. "I'm pretty sure that Leo . . . well . . . it's over and done with and he's gone. But I would like to know why it happened."

Sheree laughed, a sharp, bitter sound that held a world of pain. "Well, the first edition of the Boom-Boom girls didn't go off like Leo planned, that's for sure. I was pretty good in my day . . ."

Quill couldn't help herself. "Your day? Sheree, you're what, forty? Forty-two?"

"Oh, honey. I'm fifty-three. And don't you tell a soul. You get to a point when the docs can't help you anymore. A little lipo here, a tuck there—that'll keep the years off until you hit the big five-oh. And then . . ." she lifted her head and pointed to her neck. "Look at that." She slapped herself viciously under the chin. "Feels like a baby's diaper under there. Sloppy. No wonder

Leo fell for Brit. It's disgusting." Her lips quivered. "Not a thing I can do about it, either."

Quill put her hands to her face. There was nothing, nothing to be done about this kind of self-loathing.

"You okay, honey? Dorie said to bring you a pan quick if you needed to barf."

"I'm fine. Thanks. Shall I get us some more tea?"

"If you have some bottled water, I'd like that. Keep my system flushed out."

Quill went to her small refrigerator and brought over some Evian. "We were talking about Antonia."

"She got caught," Sheree said briefly.

"Caught?"

"You know." Sheree mimed sticking a needle into her arm. "Got into some people for some money, and ended up doing a few things she shouldn't have. She cleaned up, but by then her looks were gone. So she kind of got the shit jobs, you know? Leo ran up kind of a big bill with the people she works for and she got the job of, you know . . ." She drew a finger across her throat. "So poor Leo didn't have much of a choice."

Ruefully, Quill realized that if she were taping this conversation, Sheree hadn't actually said a single thing that could be used by a district attorney. But she knew what had happened. Antonia Caprese came to Hemlock Falls to kill Leo, at the behest of someone in Leo's organization. Leo killed Antonia before she could kill Leo. And Sheree forgave him for that.

"So Antonia followed Leo here to Hemlock Falls."

"Guess she must of."

"Sheree, why did Leo choose Hemlock Falls?"
"He knew some people here, I guess."
"By some people, do you mean Ferris Rodman?"
"I might."
"Did Ferris Rodman give Leo a hand in . . . ummm . . . Let me think of another way to phrase it. Do you think that Leo and Rodman may have met each other at the day of the fire at the MacAvoy barn?"
Sheree shrugged. But she dropped her left eyelid in a wink.
"Because Rodman was giving Leo a hand with a small job."
"That's about it."
So Rodman had helped Leo dispose of the body. "So Mr. Rodman's no stranger to violence?"
Sheree snorted, "Him? You better believe . . ." she stopped, midsentence. Her face changed. Her lips drew back. Quill had never seen anyone actually snarl before. "Rodman," she hissed. "Rodman killed Leo."
"I think so, yes."
"Why?"
It was a cry of pure anguish. It lifted the hair on Quill's head.
"I think Leo really did want to open his business here. And the village wouldn't stand for it. And that would totally blow Rodman's plans for a casino." Quill didn't want to add what she knew to be true: that the village could probably accept Rodman's promises of an upscale, elegant casino. But a neon-blazing, tacky little joint with the likes of Taffi and Candi gyrating around

barber poles would send them right off the deep end. And Quill didn't know a single person who didn't lump gambling, crime, and naked women together in an untidy heap.

Sheree sat at the kitchen table, her face hard. "Thank you," she said eventually. "It's funny, isn't it? I didn't have to go chloroforming you at all. You would have just come right out and told me."

"I told you for a specific reason, though. I don't have any proof."

"Proof?"

"Evidence. I don't even think we could get Rodman arrested."

"So we plant some. I'll help you."

"No, no, no. We can't do that."

"If the bastard killed Leo, I'd like to know why the hell not."

Quill decided to ignore this. "There's five things that link Rodman to this crime, Sheree. The wig, the uniform, the glasses, the pillow, and the phone call."

"The wig? You mean it was Rodman dressed up as that nurse."

Quill contained herself. "Yes. It was Rodman. I checked the parade-route schedule."

"The parade? Oh, you mean all those folks marching around yesterday afternoon?"

"The nurse arrived here at two o'clock, just before I came back to the Inn. The parade started at the top of Main Street—which is about a three-minute walk from the Inn. And it started at—"

"Two o'clock." Sheree nodded. "We girls were in that gift shop. Adela's Bella's or whatever. The fat lady closed it up. At first, I thought she was worried that Taff was shoplifting, which she hasn't done for months, Quill. But she hustled that big butt right off to the parade."

Quill leaned forward, intent now, on making her point. "Means, motive, and opportunity, Sheree. That's what murder is all about. Rodman was on that march. He said he was going to march at the meeting I went to earlier today. There are probably twenty people who can place him near the Inn at the relevant time. So he had the opportunity."

Quill sat back. "We know the motive; Norrie can attest to the fact that Leo was actually planning to open Lovejoy's, and that he didn't care how much money Rodman offered him. What we don't have is the means."

"The means," Sheree said. "Like, a gun?"

"Yes. The murder weapon is usually the means. We have the actual weapon. It was one of the pillows in the suite. I'm talking about the 'means' that allowed Rodman into the Inn disguised as the nurse. That's what we have to get. The disguise. There'll be forensics evidence all over those clothes. And Rodman knows it."

"But nobody saw Rodman himself, did they? The only person who came in here that was new was that nurse. You mean Rodman was that nurse." She was talking to herself, rather than Quill. She looked as bewildered as a child. "I let him in!" she cried out, stricken. "And I left Leo alone with the murderer!"

"We have a chance to get him," Quill said. "We just have to get the evidence."

"So we need to sneak into Rodman's house and find a wig, some glasses, a uniform, and a what?"

"A pillow. It was the quickest way to stuff the uniform. I'll bet you anything it was a goose-down pillow from the Inn. But no, we aren't going to march into his house. We won't find those things, Sheree. Rodman's not stupid. He's buried them, or burned them, or got ridden of them somehow. What we have to do is trick his accomplice into thinking we've got them."

"I don't get it."

Quill sighed. This was actually the hardest part. But Sheree would have to know, sooner or later.

"The wig, the pillow, and the spectacles came from the Inn. So did the phone call that alerted Rodman that Dina had called the nursing service. There are three people who were in a position to deliver all those things. But only one with the opportunity to do it. You and Taffi and Candi were at the parade yesterday. One person was alone with Leo and Norrie. It would have been easy for her to slip out of the suite and leave the two of them together, playing cards while she slipped the wig and the glasses to Rodman."

"Brittney-Anne!"

CHAPTER 14

"I don't think I can stand this," Sheree whispered. "What if the bastard doesn't show up?"

Quill gently put her hand over Sheree's mouth and whispered back, "We're not supposed to be here. If Davy hears you, he'll arrest us both."

They crouched in the willows near the statue of General C.C. Hemlock in the center of Peterson Park. Quill's knees hurt. Brittney-Anne Maltby sat sullenly on the bench under the weak streetlight that illuminated the general and his horse. She was huddled into a silver Lurex sweater. It was after midnight, and the air was cool for August.

"You don't have to be here," Sheree hissed furiously.

"I couldn't let you go alone."

Sheree's hands clutched hers. They were icy cold. Quill squeezed them encouragingly.

An engine purred up the dirt path that led to the village. There were no headlights. There was the quiet snick of an opening door. Then footsteps on the gravel.

Ferris Rodman walked into the glow of the streetlight. Quill's breath caught somewhere in her chest. That morning, Quill and Sheree had driven to Ithaca and gotten another gray wig, a size-sixteen nurse's uniform, and a pair of heart-rimmed glasses just like the ones Meg had worn to disguise herself at Seasons in the Sun. Quill had (reluctantly) sacrificed another of the expensive goose-down pillows. Then they had rolled the whole bundle in the compost pile and presented the newly discovered "evidence" to Brittney-Anne. The only tough part had been to convince Agent Purvis to come with them when they confronted her. (An indirect reference to his aversion to corpses, and Lieutenant Parker, had helped. Quill's conscience still stung her about that one.) Davy had proved more than competent to take Brittney-Anne's confession from there, and she agreed to call Rodman and demand money for her silence.

"Where is the money?" Brittney-Anne demanded now. "You want me to keep quiet about you killing that little son of a bitch, you'd better have brought it."

"Oh, you're going to keep quiet about my killing that little son of a bitch," Rodman said.

"Well," Davy Kiddermeister said as he stepped out from the brush nearby. "I guess you're under arrest, Mr. Rodman."

CHAPTER 15

"But, what about Arnold Schwarzenegger?" Adela wailed.

"Adela," Elmer said, with a remarkable show of firmness. "I don't think Arnold Schwarzenegger was planning on showing up in the first place."

Elmer had returned to run the Chamber meetings. And the Chamber was meeting at the Inn again. So there were two good results stemming from the arrest of

Ferris Rodman for the murder of Leo "Boom-Boom" Maltby.

Quill shifted in her chair. She hadn't noticed how hard the seat was before. The chairs at the Resort were much more comfortable than the ones at the Inn. But the Resort was closed "for the duration" according to the mayor, and the Chamber meetings were going to be held at the Inn again, for the duration. Quill wondered how long a duration was. She'd have to look it up. She also wondered if they could afford to buy Ferris Rodman's chairs. He'd have to sell something to pay for his defense. Howie Murchison had told them all ROCOR had filed for Chapter Eleven at nine o'clock that morning.

The Conference Room was so full that some people had to stand in the hall. Quill saw Chamber members she hadn't seen for years. She leaned across Howie Murchison and spoke to Miriam Doncaster. "This is more of a town meeting than an emergency Chamber session. Maybe we should move to the Town Hall?"

Miriam made a face. "Those chairs are worse than yours. And there's no air conditioning. Your air conditioning isn't what I'd call state of the art, but at least it moves the air around."

"Thanks," Quill said dubiously.

Harland Peterson took the floor. "So we don't know if the Resort's just going to sit there, or what?" His broad face held disgust. Nothing got under the skin of the Hemlock Falls farmer more than waste. "Government's got a lot to answer for."

There was a murmur of agreement.

"Government's got nothing to do with it," Marge Schmidt said. "Damn bank's got a lot to do with it, though. What damn fool kept lending Rodman money?"

"Order, order," Elmer said, tapping the gavel. "We've got to vote on a couple of things, yet. You got the minutes from last meeting, Quill?"

"Actually, Miriam has them," Quill said apologetically. "I didn't think I was secretary anymore."

"What the hey," Elmer said. "Who told you that?" His gaze drifted to his wife. He stuck his lower lip out and stood a moment, clearly considering his next words. "Some change is good change," he said, with unexpected kindness. "But mostly I think we should keep things the way they are. We would appreciate it very much if you would continue in your job as our secretary, Quill."

Applause shook the table. Quill was seriously discomposed. She didn't want to be secretary of the Hemlock Falls Chamber of Commerce. And she was terrible at it. She'd developed a shorthand that nobody could read, including herself. She covered the minutes pages with drawings because she was constitutionally unable to hold a pencil for any length of time without sketching. And she'd been trying to get rid of the job for years. She stood up and bowed slightly. "Thank you very much. I'd be honored. Thank you."

Hands passed Miriam's notebook to her. Miriam sent her a smile and a thumbs up.

"So," Elmer said, "Could we have a reading of the last meeting's minutes?"

Quill stared at Miriam's note-taking. Everything was neatly labeled: OLD BUSINESS; NEW BUSINESS; FOR FILE; FOR FOLLOWUP. Underneath each caption were neat bulleted items. She'd even written "submitted by Miriam Doncaster. MLS," and the date. Quill looked at Miriam. Miriam mouthed "no way."

"I think the first item of business," Elmer said, ignoring his own dictum, "should be this referendum on Lovejoy's Nudie Bar and Grill. I've been in touch with Mr. Norwood Ferguson, and he has agreed, reluctantly, to sell the town the MacAvoy property."

Marge frowned. "How much is he asking for it?"

Quill got up and excused herself. Sheree and the remaining Boom-Boom girls were checking out of the Inn at eleven. It was nearly that now.

They were standing by the receptionist desk when Quill got there. Sheree was talking earnestly to Dina. She looked up as Quill came in and gave her a wan smile. She was drawn and her face was pale despite the makeup. For the first time, Quill believed she was in her fifties. "Come to see us off, honey?"

Quill gave her a quick hug. "Wouldn't miss it. Is your luggage all taken care of?"

"That cute guy Mike put it in the van for us. We're going to catch the twelve o'clock train to New York.

"And what will you do then?"

"Oh, Norrie'll find us a gig. He's gone up ahead, to find us a little apartment. We'll be fine. You heard that Oprah cancelled?"

"I did. Meg told me. I'm so sorry."

"Your sister's pretty sweet, honey. We had a nice long chat this morning while you were sleeping in."

"I wish you could have gotten some rest, too, Sheree."

Her eyes were shadowed. "Just couldn't settle down. I'm so glad we nailed that guy. I'm going to remember that for the rest of my life. I'm going to remember you for the rest of my life."

Quill, who was always helpless in the face of compliments, lifted her hands and let them drop again.

"You know, while Leo was alive, I always knew that someday we'd get back together again. Gave a girl something to look forward to. 'Cause that's all that counts in the end, honey. Somebody to love and look forward to." She gave Quill's wrist a little shake. "You remember that."

"You're sure you three won't stay for the wedding?"

"Ah." Tears glittered in her eyes. "You're sweet, too. No. We have to move on." She turned to Taffi and Candi. Taffi had just finished telling Dina something that left the receptionist open-mouthed and giggling. "You leave that kid alone, girls. Shake it on out to the van, now." She turned at the door. "Bye, Quill. You take care of your sister."

"I always have."

Quill went to the door and watched as the van drove slowly away.

"Wow," Dina said.

"So are you ready to leave this boring receptionist job · the bright lights, big city?"

Are you kidding me? To borrow a phrase from Meg, rather eat a rat.' It's back to the copepods for me."

ood. And speaking of Meg . . ."

"In the kitchen. But before you go find her, you'd better see this."

"What? What is it?"

"This week's edition of the *Hemlock Falls Gazette.*"

Quill took the paper. "This is the headline about Leo's murder and Ferris Rodman's arrest and Brittney-Anne's plea bargain. I can't tell you how much I don't want to read about Leo's murder."

"Not that. Page three."

Quill folded the front page over. The top of page three had a banner headline: PEPPERCORN: A CRITICAL REVIEW by Jacques Fromage.

"Oh my god. It's Meg's first column!"

Quill crushed the paper closed and stared at Dina in dismay. "It says, 'this week, M. Fromage visits Seasons in the Sun.' I can't read it Dina. I can't. I was looking forward to a nice, peaceful day and then the wedding tomorrow. The last thing we need is a chef war."

"A chef war?"

"You know Stoke. He loves controversy. He says it's good for the paper. It is good for the paper. But it's terrible for me! I'll bet you anything he's on the phone to Jerry Grimsby right now. 'How's about a little reply' he'll ask, and next week's *Gazette* will have Crackecorn: The REPLY! by Madame Guillotine, or whatever. And they won't stop until they're both dead."

"Just read it," Dina said mildly. "It's good."

"I'm sure it's more than good. I'm sure it's brilliant. Nobody knows food like my sister."

"I never thought you were, like, a coward."

"Fine!" Quill snapped. "I'll read the darn thing. She read it.

And Dina was right. It was a brilliant piece of critical work. Wasted, Quill thought guiltily, on their little, small-town paper. If anyone from the trade magazines saw this, they'd be on Meg like a shot, begging her to write for them.

She finished the article. Dina made a "high-five" gesture with one hand. Thoughtfully, Quill walked to the kitchen.

There was already a small amount of early trade in the dining room. Quill noticed the Chef's Special on the blackboard next to the maître 'd's lectern:

DUCK GRIMSBY

She pushed the swinging doors to the dining room open. Jerry and Meg were standing side by side at the prep table, elbows touching. They were both staring at a sauté pan filled with something aromatic. It featured shrimp.

"I told you saffron was a stupid choice," Meg said.

"And you turned out to be right. So what?"

"So say it."

"You're right." He looked at her. Quill's heart lurched not because of Jerry's look, which she seen before, but at Meg's soft-eyed glow. "You're right, Meg," and looked for a moment as if he'd kiss her.

Quill left without making her presence known. She went back to the foyer. "I'll be up in my room for a while, if anyone wants me."

"Well, that's good, because guess who just walked in?" Dina said smugly.

"I don't care if it's the Dalai Lama," Quill said crossly. "I just want a little time to myself. Okay?"

"Fine by me."

Max lay outside her door, waiting to get in. "Why aren't you out trashing Dumpsters?" She bent down and rumpled his ears. "You're never in at this time of day, Maxie. Unless . . ." Suddenly, she knew who'd just walked in the door. She opened the door and called, "Myles!"

He emerged from the bedroom. He'd loosened his tie and his dress shirt was open at the throat. He looked wonderful. She crossed the space between them in two long strides threw herself into his arms. "You don't *know* how glad I am to see you."

His kissed her, hard. "And I'm glad to see you in one piece."

"Davy called you."

"John actually. I would have been back yesterday if it'd been Davy. John seemed to think things were well in hand."

"And he's got pretty good judgment."

"One of the best. We could use him in my line of work. Wish he'd consider it."

"They've got a baby coming!" Quill said.

"There is that." He looked at her, his eyes silver with unexpressed concern. "How do you feel?"

She breathed into her palm. "Can you still smell it?"

"The chloroform? Yes. Highly unpleasant."

"I still feel a little punky."

"There are a lot of reasons why no one uses chloroform as an anesthetic anymore. Feeling punky for days is one of them." He turned to go back into the bedroom. His scarred and battered duffle bag was on the bed, the contents in a neat pile on the floor. He stripped off his dress shirt. Quill ran her hands across his chest. "Only three scars."

"Same number as before."

"Thank goodness." She didn't ask where he'd been or what he had been doing. She sat down and waited until he'd changed into chinos and a tee-shirt.

"Other than your successful capture of Ferris Rodman, is there any news?"

"How much time will he do, Myles?"

"You really don't like this guy."

"I really don't." She frowned. "You know why? It's because it was essentially a passionless crime. I mean, he had a passion for money, I guess. But greed's no substitute for feelings about people. He didn't care at all about people. You know what he said when Davy arrested him?"

Myles shook his head.

" 'Had to be done.' And then he shrugged. I'll tell you something. I'm glad Sheree didn't have a gun. She would have shot him dead. And if he had killed you, Myles, and said that to me, I would have shot him dead. And I can't tell you how much I disapprove of murder."

Myles put his head down and laughed.

"Okay," she said tolerantly. "Go ahead and laugh. But I'm so glad you're home I can't even begin to say it. I was afraid you wouldn't make it."

"And miss Meg's wedding?"

"Meg's wedding," Quill said. She rubbed her arms, as if she were cold. "I don't think there's going to be a wedding, Myles."

"No?"

"You're not surprised."

"No. I'm not surprised. I think Andy's more involved with Meg than she with him. She's terrified of hurting him. And like a lot of people in similar situations, she's avoiding facing it. And I think . . ." He stopped to pull on his Docksiders.

"That she's terrified of disappointing me?"

"Yes."

"All I want is her happiness!" Quill cried, even as she realized it was the balked cry of thousands of loving, (but interfering) mothers, aunts, sisters, and best friends. "You know, for a long time, all we had was each other. Literally. Our parents left us more than enough money. I've told you that. We could afford to hire a housekeeper after our parents died, and we did. And when I went off to NYU, I moved Meg into the city and we lived near campus together. There was a succession of housekeepers and eventually, Aunt Eleanor, but always, always, Myles, there was the two of us. And I was the older one and the calmer one and the responsible one."

Myles came and sat down next to her.

"And you want to hand her over to someone just as calm and responsible."

"Andy. And before him, Daniel."

"And?"

"Jerry Grimsby," she said between her teeth, "hasn't held a steady job in years. Do you know what the life of a professional chef is like? I mean, he's bounced all over the continent. And he's not serious!"

Myles put his arm around her. "You feel better?"

"Much."

"Do you really dislike Grimsby?"

"No," Quill said without thinking. "I like him a lot."

"Does he love Meg?"

"Better than oatmeal," Quill said flippantly. "Better than raisins. Better than anything in this life, if I'm any judge."

His grip tightened. "And are you? A good judge of someone who loves you better than anything in this life?"

"But Myles . . . what about the wedding?"

He took a deep breath. "I have an idea about that."

"This dress is too short!" Quill said.

Meg stepped back and tilted her head to one side. "It's

not too short. It was too long on me. It's tea length on you. The silver and rose look great with your hair. Perfect for a summer afternoon wedding."

Quill ran her hands down the sides of the silk. Meg handed her the bouquet. Wisteria and ivy spilled over her hands. "I feel like a priestess in some weird, antiquated ritual. Is everyone out there?"

Meg looked through the glass doors in the Tavern Lounge out to the lawn. The gazebo perched over the Falls was draped with more wisteria and the ivy waved gently in the breeze.

"Doreen, Dina, Davy, Kathleen, Marge, and Harland. They're all there, Sis. And Dookie and Mrs. Dookie, of course."

"And Myles," Quill asked suddenly panicked.

"Always Myles," Meg said.

And Quill stepped out onto the velvet green lawn, to the sound of the singing falls.

DUCK GRIMSBY

Meg, of course, loved Jerry's Duck Grimsby. And she's right: duck is a huge challenge to a chef. And it's not because duck recipes are complicated to prepare; it's because successful duck lies in the technique used to prepare the duck and in the choice of sauces to complement the duck's special flavor. It is all too easy to prepare duck that tastes just like chicken.

Ingredients
1 sprig fresh rosemary
1 clove garlic, thinly sliced
2 tbsps extra virgin olive oil
2 tbsps French butter, melted
4 wild duck breasts, boned and trimmed

Combine the first four ingredients into a marinade. Dry the breasts with paper towels. Coat the breasts with the marinade. Place in a glass bowl, cover with a cloth dishtowel and marinate in the refrigerator overnight.

CHUTNEY
Chutneys are pungent condiments. They are normally fruit-based. This variation on Jerry's recipe features mangos.

Ingredients
6 green mangoes, peeled and sliced
1 cup red wine vinegar
1 cup dark brown sugar
10 cloves garlic, peeled and sliced
1 inch peeled, sliced ginger root
1 tsp ground red chilis
1 tsp salt

Simmer all ingredients for thirty minutes.

Broil the duck breasts under high heat for 6 to 8 minutes. Skin should be crisp and slightly charred, and the meat of the duck medium-pink. Serve with warmed chutney.

BETTY HALL'S GARBAGE PLATE

We don't know if Arnold Schwarzennegger would have come all the way from California to eat this or not, but it is a highly popular item in upstate New York diners.

Assemble one white-hot with grilled bun, one red-hot with grilled bun, one grilled hamburger with grilled bun, one scoop baked beans, and one scoop cole slaw on a very large plate. Serve with ketchup, mustard, onions, and sweet-and-sour pickles.

Baked Beans

1 large can of Grandma Brown's baked beans
3 slices maple-cured, thick-sliced bacon
1 large onion, chopped
1 cup dark brown sugar

Assemble ingredients in casserole. Slow-bake for three hours at 250 degrees.

Cole Slaw

1 head garden-fresh green cabbage, grated
1 large carrot, grated
1 sweet (Vidalia or Maya) onion, grated
1 large green pepper, diced into small squares

Mix into large glass bowl.

Dressing
2 cups Miracle Whip
1 cup cider vinegar
2 to 4 tablespoons white sugar to taste

Whip all ingredients together and mix with greens.

Center Point Publishing
600 Brooks Road • PO Box 1
Thorndike ME 04986-0001 USA

(207) 568-3717

US & Canada:
1 800 929-9108